CHRISTMAS

STORIES

CHRISTMAS STORIES

George Mackay Brown

Edited and with an Introduction
by
William S. Peterson

Galileo Publishers

Published by Galileo Publishers
16 Woodlands Road, Great Shelford, Cambridge, UK, CB22 5LW
www.galileopublishing.co.uk
Galileo Publishers is an imprint of Galileo Multimedia Ltd.

USA: SCB Distributors
15608 S. New Century Drive, Gardena, CA 90248-2129 | USA

Australia: Peribo Pty Ltd
58 Beaumont Rd, Mount Kuring-Gai, 2080 NSW | Australia

ISBN: 9781912916535

The Publishers thank the Estate of George Mackay Brown for
their permission to reproduce these stories.

Cover illustration © John Lawrence
Interior illustrations:
© Rosemary Roberts & © John Lawrence

Printed in the EU

Contents

Introduction

In the autobiographical essay (its title deliberately echoing Dylan Thomas's 'A Child's Christmas in Wales') that opens this collection of Christmas stories, George Mackay Brown recalls the heavy hand of Presbyterianism on Orkney during his childhood: 'no images or candles to brighten the dark time,' 'no crib in the kirk,' 'no pubs where the old seamen and fishermen could go and tell their winter stories.' Yet despite the laments on other occasions about his 'Knox-ruined nation,' still haunted by a grey Calvinism, Brown was delighted to witness, during his own lifetime, a gentle revival of traditional Yule festivities, and he emphasized in all his tales that Christmas did not consist of merely a one-day celebration of the birth of Christ. It was in fact the centre of an annual observance of wintry delights: the prolonged anticipation of the Advent season (which begins on the Sunday closest to 30 November), the joyous family activities of Christmas Eve and Christmas Day, the convivial First Footing of Hogmanay (New Year's Eve), and finally Epiphany (6 January), associated with the biblical story of the Magi and their visit to the Christ child. In Brown's stories, we see an intricate mixture of scriptural traditions, medieval legends, and modern folk customs, all reaching backward toward the prehistoric rituals of the winter solstice.

On a cluster of small northern islands where the Atlantic and the North Sea send waves crashing into the shoreline, surrounded by profound winter blackness, Brown's fictional characters find themselves compelled to re-enact the Christmas story. The allegorical landscape is populated by fishermen and shepherds (thus echoing the world of the Gospels), and in many of his tales we hear about a mysterious infant, bathed in rays of light, who is concealed in a local byre. Brown often describes three enigmatic strangers, with exotic clothing and manners, who have come in search of that child. We are never allowed to gaze directly at Jesus – the illumination would perhaps be too dazzling for our eyes – but frequently in the stories we are conscious of his supernatural presence in a dark, deserted cowshed.

It was not merely gloomy Scottish Calvinism that for centuries banished the social and spiritual delights of the midwinter season; Brown also views with suspicion the pretensions of modern science. A few of his characters (Alastair Lorne in 'Stars,' for example) are eager to stamp out superstition and embrace mathematics and rationality as the key to understanding an enigmatic universe, but in the end, Brown tells us, it is the very young, as well as the isolated eccentrics of Orkney, who, through intuition and simple faith, display a deeper understanding of the cosmos around them. Similarly, he suggests (in 'A Candle for Milk and Grass') that our confidence in modern technology is delusional: it makes our lives superficially more comfortable but cuts us off from the profound truths of earth, sea, and sky.

In reading Brown's Christmas tales, we must remember that, from his point of view, chronology is essentially meaningless. Some of them are set in the ancient or medieval world; others seem to be taking place in the early twentieth century. Always, however, he insists upon collapsing the distinction between the present and a shadowy past, and we are constantly made aware of the deepest, most recurrent truths of human existence. Despite the incursions of the modern world, his Orkney is populated by men, women, and children quietly re-enacting the rituals of Neolithic and Viking forebears who once lived there. George Mackay Brown wants to remind us that when we, in the darkness of winter, recite again those tales of a child born in an abandoned shed, attended by kneeling shepherds and kings, we are reconnecting with the most elemental forces of the universe.

William S. Peterson, Washington, DC, July 2020

A Child's Christmas

It was a magic time for us children, though nearly every family in the little fishing town was poor.

Winter was darker and longer than any other place in Britain. We were not to know that.

It was a Presbyterian town, so there were no images or candles to brighten the dark time. Certainly there was no crib in the kirk.

There were no pubs where the old seamen and fishermen could go and tell their winter stories. Story-telling, in one form or another, had been the great art of the islands, for thousands of years, reaching a pure narrative form in the Norse sagas. (We children knew nothing about that either.) The many pubs along the street had been voted out of existence about the time I was born – the appalled townsfolk had witnessed such scenes of drunkenness and violence during the war, between the Irish labourers and the English marines.

There was seemingly nothing to cause excitement and joy. Yet the current of laughter and expectation began to flow from early December on.

I ought to have said that, a generation earlier, in my father's time, Christmas was an ordinary day, with all the shops open and business going on at counter and office. There was no overt anti-Catholic feeling in Orkney when I was a boy; there were only two Catholics in our town, an Italian café owner and an Irish barber, and they were accepted as equals. But in the centuries since the Reformation, Orkney (that had once been a devout Catholic place) had been well steeped in the greyness of Presbyterianism. It may be that the very name Christmas evoked uneasiness in some minds: it was as often referred to as Yule. Many islanders regarded Hogmanay, a week later, as the real winter feast.

The excitement began with the stories, the birth in the byre with the ox and the ass, the three kings and the star, the angels and shepherds. Such images and wonders enthralled us, even in the Presbyterian Sunday-school where we first heard them.

And in our strict Scottish day-school, there was a little relaxation. The chains of word and number dropped from us; we stood for hours with strips of coloured paper and pots of paste, making paper chains instead. And oh, the wonder when, a day or two before the school broke up, those paper chains were hung along the school walls! The grim cavern of the classroom became suddenly a bazaar, a fair, a palace.

'You must write a letter to Santa,' said my sister, 'telling him what you want.' I forget what most boys desired in those days. But the letter to Santa Claus was written and sent up the chimney. An updraught might whirl it up among the stars; more often than not it dropped back, sooty and scorched, on to the hearth. That did not worry me – in some mysterious way the kind old white-bearded man in the red coat with the toy factory at the North Pole had got the message. He would find his way down that same chimney a few nights later.

The little living-room was decorated, with penny decorations, and there was always a paper bell at the centre of the display. A sprig of mistletoe was nailed to a rafter. To be given a sudden kiss 'under the mistletoe' meant that the man or woman so saluted had to buy a gift to the bold kisser. There was great laughter whenever some prim lady who had not been kissed all year was caught unawares. And if she joined in the delight, it was all the merrier.

Christmas cards were just beginning when I was young. A family might receive a half-dozen or so; they were rather ugly, with celluloid facings and florid silvery script, more like funeral cards than greetings. They were set in a solemn row along the mantelpiece, among the tea-caddies and the china dogs.

My mother made 'Crestona' ginger wine, bottle upon bottle. I have never tasted better draughts of vintage.

How did I ever manage to sleep on Christmas Eve? The young men of the town had hacked down a tree in some garden, by stealth. The two divisions of the town under the ringing stars, strove mightily to drag 'the Yule log' to this or that mark of victory.

Festival or famine, sleep will come to a child. But there's a bell inside his head that wakes him early on Christmas morning. The stocking at the end of the bed is a dark loaded bulk. No pirate ever unlocked treasure-chest with such enraptured fingers. I found none of the wealth that a modern child expects from glaring into spangled multi-store windows or into television screens. Very likely, Santa's factory was no longer making the things I had mentioned in my letter. There was always an apple and an orange and a bag of sweets, and either a book or a game of ludo or a toy, and perhaps a sixpence that shone like a star in the lamplight. I have not known, since, such surges of happiness.

The same thing was happening in a hundred bedrooms all over Hamnavoe.

We did not know that the long darkness of the year was over, and that the tide had set sunwards. The Incarnation was a theological concept that we knew nothing about. We were content with the marvellous stories and the carols – the toy factory at the North Pole – the soundless paper bell and the mistletoe – the fire in the range and the paraffin lamp that was lit in mid-afternoon – and the joyful faces that came and went all day.

The Lost Sheep

The island had been empty of people for fifty years.

There were a dozen ruins scattered here and there in the island. The sheep sheltered behind those walls in bad weather. I went every summer to shear the flock, and in the autumn to sail them across to Hamnavoe, to the mart there. If possible, I crossed over in the motorboat at lambing time. The weather is often bad at this time of the year, and I have a big farm to run.

If ewes and lambs survive, it is some years the old wisdom of nature that preserves them. More than once, I have found what has been left − a few rags of fleece, a few bones − by the skuas and the hoodie crows.

It is a melancholy island to be in, even for an afternoon. Men and women lived there once that are still spoken about in the other islands for some marvellous thing said or done. There was one famous fiddler. There was a horseman who was sent for from as far away as Shetland and Caithness whenever there were intractable horses. There was the woman who could foretell the weather a month ahead: the fishermen in the island saw to it that she was never short of haddocks and skate. (But at the same time they said, 'Three hundred years ago Meg would have been burned for a witch.')

There had even been a marvellous child in the island, once. In the summer of drought, four or five generations ago, when no rain fell all over Orkney between seed-time and harvest – 'the summer of the short corn,' it was called – this six-year-old boy went to a stony part of the island and he said, 'They should dig here.' They dug, and water came up sweet and cold.

Those things, and a hundred more, were still remembered about that island, in the fertile islands that lay all about it.

When the last family had left the island, my grandfather had bought it for one hundred pounds, every stone and clod, every shell and seaweed frond down to the lowest ebb. And there my grandfather and my father and now myself grazed a few sheep.

One afternoon, ten years ago and more, I sheltered from a shower in the ruins of the smithy. There was the blackened forge, still. The anvil had been too valuable to leave behind. A few horseshoes hung here and there against the walls. There was a scattering of nails on the bench. I was struck by the shine and sharpness of the nails – they could still have been used for roof-timbers or to build a boat.

I thought, 'Here the island men came together on winter nights to tell their stories.' The stories of that island have passed into the great silence. Something delicate and unique and rich – the spirit of the island – died when Willie the blacksmith closed his door for the last time.

Brightness seeped through the webbed window of the smithy. I could see gray cinders in the forge. The shower was past. I went down in sunshine to my boat on the shore.

★ ★ ★

There is a retired sailor who rents a small bothy from me down at the shore. He spends most of the time – when he isn't in the village inn drinking – scanning the horizon through his brass telescope.

I don't have much to do with old Ben: he is one of those ancient mariners who tell, over and over, his experiences at sea since he first joined a trawler at Hamnavoe at the age of fifteen. There are about twenty stories in his repertoire. A man gets weary of listening to them over and over again – at least I do. Ben is made welcome at most houses, but he visits most often the farms and crofts where they brew their own ale. So I rarely see him, except when I go down to the bothy to collect the rent.

The winter last year was cold and stormy.

The first television sets had come to the island. They were the latest of the never-ending miracles of science, those half-dozen television sets lately installed in the bigger farms. They held children from their play and old men from their memories in the chimney corner. The poorer folk who couldn't afford to buy television sets would almost beg to spend their evenings in those fortunate houses where the gray images flickered and came and went.

I'm glad to say that the enchantment didn't last. The islanders came to the conclusion that there was probably more fun playing draughts on the kitchen table by lamplight. The fiddle was taken down from the wall again. Cherished books were brought from the wide windowsill and opened with reverence and delight. But while it lasted, even Ben the sailor was under the spell of the television set, going from this house to that.

My wife and three children, I know, would have welcomed

a set in our house. I answered their unspoken pleas with a hard look, and silence.

★   ★   ★

The gales began in late October and seemed to follow each other, with only brief interludes, going in a great wheel through the twelve quarters during November and well into the first half of December. The sun is a dying ember at that time of year in the north. People come out of the bitter winds and gather round those small providences of the sun, the peat-fires on the hearth, the mild radiance of the lamps. (But here again, I'm sorry to say, in most island houses nowadays they get electric light and warmth from the wind generators at the gable-end of the barn.)

There came a knock at the door late one morning. There was a lull that day in the winter-long storm. The sky was a pale blue, but there were battlements of blue-black cloud on the horizon westwards, and that meant snow. The low sun flashed off a quiet sea.

When Ben came in, there were a few snowflakes in his hand. He was carrying his brass telescope.

My wife hastened to make tea for the visitor.

'No,' said Ben, 'I can't stay. I just came to say, one of your sheep in the island has gone over the cliff. She seems all right but there's no way for her to get back.'

Normally, on a winter afternoon, with darkness due and snow clouds threatening, I would have left the ewe to nature. Let her find her own way to the top. If not — it had happened before, it would happen again. Nature is cruel.

In the end I followed the old sailor down to the shore.

I pushed out the boat, started the motor, and went in a wide arc along the tide-rip to the edge of the small cove in the deserted island. I went at once to the part of the cliff where the ewe had gone over. There was no sign of it on any of the crag-ledges. It had likely lost its footing and fallen into the sea.

The cold sun stood just over the southeast horizon. The snow cloud had come up quickly from the west, and before I knew it I was enveloped in a blizzard. The crystal of the day was broken — a wind began to sough among the barren whin bushes. I was happy about the wind at least. It meant that the snow clouds would be kept on the move. I would not be exiled on the island by a day-long blizzard. I could get home by the light of sunset, or even, if I had to wait that long, by the stars.

Meantime the snow was falling thicker. I would have to shelter, like the flock, behind some wall.

A ruin loomed through the murk, the church.

I assure you, no one has visited the island except myself all this past year. It is a small hump in the sea, that island. Every movement on it is visible from my house across the Sound.

A fire had been lit some time that day against the east wall of the kirk. I could smell the incense of still-smouldering peat. There it was, a fire-black stone with warm ash on it.

There had been a meal too, of a kind. Alongside the fire were the bones of two fish — haddock — and five crusts from a torn loaf.

On the other side of the fire-stone three coins had been left — a shilling, a sixpence, and a penny.

They were honest guests, whoever they were. This payment, I thought, must be for the use of the sanctuary. By right the coins were mine, but I thought it better to leave them there, under the last light and the snow.

As I stood in the kirk porch, the big snow cloud had moved off eastward, and the first star was out over the Atlantic. The air was quiet again. But another blue-black battlement was building up on the western horizon. There would be more snow before midnight. It was cold. I walked quickly down to the boat at the shore.

Ben Smith had stuck a candle in a bottle in his window. It looked more festive, that flame, than the tinsel-coloured Christmas lights in this farm window and that.

No doubt the sailor had spied all my movements that day on the island of sheep. He came down to meet me. Did I expect to hear a story of some strangers on my island, winter trespassers, and where had they come from, and how had they gotten on to the island, and what did they want there at this time of year? Surely he had seen something through that lucid prism.

All Ben said was, 'A good Yule to you, mister.'

I went on past him without a word, up to my farm that had no tree in the window.

Herman: A Christmas Story

I

Legion CCIV occupied forts that winter in the German Alps.

A hard bitter time that was.

The Germans attacked again and again, through blizzards, ice, and thaws. There was little rest.

A sortie was made against a German village. Many villagers were killed, others fled. A boy was taken back, a prisoner: his name Herman.

They put Herman to such work as sweeping and scouring bronze in the barracks.

Then word came that three companies of the legion were to be withdrawn, to some unspecified post in the low countries westward.

That day the colonel Maximinius was beside himself with joy. Even the ordinary soldiers had a ration of wine instead of beer that day.

II

Herman stood on the coast in Belgium looking at the sea for the first time.

The brimming and shrinking of the sea twice a day filled him with astonishment, and also one bleak gray storm that sent combers high up the sand, and also the marvellous calm that brooded on the ocean on days of hard frost.

The colonel stood all one morning looking across at Britannia. 'It may be we are going there, among the fogs and marshes,' said Maximinius to the officers. 'I pray not. We must wait for the captain of the convoy.'

The troopships did not come till the second half of the month.

The captain was entertained in his tent by the colonel. The colonel and some senior officers dined on shipboard.

Still no word came of their destination.

'Polish my greaves,' said Maximinius to the orderly in the door of the tent.

By now Herman knew some Latin words.

The colonel wore bright harness to entertain the marine officers that night. The captain had only vague news. He would break the seal on the official letter at dawn. Embarkation would take place in the morning.

The captain did not know the destination, other than that he must clear the northwest coast of Gaul, and hold south.

'This is no time of year, late winter,' said Maximinius to the convoy commander, 'to move troops by sea.'

The ships, one by one, up-anchored. Herman staggered all about the deck with the first movements of ship on water.

III

They anchored in a Spanish harbour. They hoped to take on board wine, olives, and citrus fruits.

The town was empty and the trading booths shuttered.

Either the people had evacuated the town on sighting the convoy and taken to the mountains, or else the place had been bled dry by bandits.

'Does the sea go on for ever?' asked Herman.

'Yes,' said Phocas the Greek corporal, 'the sea girdles the earth, a bright garment. The sea is mother of all.'

In Spain there was bad feeling between the colonel and the captain of the ships.

Some soldiers, a chosen band, had made a sortie into the forest and returned driving cattle and swine; the sailors held that in the share-out they had come off badly.

The soldiers' feast-fires burned on the shore for three nights.

'You are to embark the troops in the morning,' said the captain to the colonel, the words written and sealed and delivered by hand. 'The ships will sail at noon.'

Herman helped to cover the feast fires.

'The Spanish cattle are too lean,' said Herman.

IV

A storm in Biscay drove the convoy hither and thither, this way and that, most of the month of April.

Many of the soldiers were sick in that long westerly storm. A few died and were dropped, weighted, into the Atlantic.

The sailors stood up to the buffeting better than the soldiers. There was mockery from oars and masts at the soldiers' misery.

For two watches Herman was so ill that he longed for death.

15

'What a green face!' said Phocas the corporal. 'The wind's in the north now and we're being driven round Africa. Cheer up, German. We might see lions and men with black faces.'

The wind shifted into the east and blew the fleet westward till it was out of sight of Africa.

The colonel sent word to the captain that, if more legionaries died, the captain would have to render account to the senate in Rome. The senate (the letter went on) would want to know why they had not sought a safe harbour until the storm blew itself out.

The captain made no reply to that letter.

Then the wind swung south and west, and moderated, and the ships sailed through the Pillars of Hercules into the Roman Sea.

'I saw neither lion nor elephant,' said Herman.

V

In Tripoli they shipped a great cargo of wheat, wine, salt beef and olives. Their stores had been much depleted.

Some of the soldiers and one or two sailors deserted in North Africa.

The colonel Maximinius complained to the captain about that, in a sealed letter. The ships had been too long in port, he wrote.

This time the captain replied. 'There are always desertions in ports with taverns and women. I will recruit sailors from the dockers, as always. I advise you to do likewise. Black Africans will make you brave troopers. As for the loading, it is being effected with utmost despatch.'

The colonel did not reply to that letter.

Several Africans were recruited or taken by force to be sailors.

Herman saw black men for the first time. He wondered at those black faces out of which the sun seemed to shine. The new black sailors were always laughing and dancing.

'The future belongs to them,' said Phocas the Greek to Herman. 'In Greece and Rome we have given up natural joy for power and profit. Our civilisation is worn thin like an old coin.'

The ships were seaborne again.

A letter from the colonel to the captain: 'As soon as I am set ashore at Ostia, I will make a true account of this voyage. I have friends in the Civil Service and in the Senate.'

The captain held this letter in the flame of his lantern. He laughed.

It began to be hot in the ships.

'This sea smells,' said Herman. 'I liked better the great ocean. Better still I liked the mountains in Germany.'

The ships sailed on past the toe of Italy, and on east.

VI

The heat of the summer was moderated by a dense fog that lasted for two weeks.

The ships drifted on lost and blind.

The ship Francia on which Herman sailed lost touch with the main fleet.

One day they saw ships looming out of the fog but they knew at once that they were not their ships for these ships were smaller and lighter and they looked like sea scorpions.

The three pirate vessels attacked Francia with arrows and missiles but the soldiers kept them away with spears.

Some of the pirates got a rope over the stern of Francia and 20 of them clambered on to the deck, with knives in their teeth.

There was an hour-long struggle before the last of the pirates who hadn't been killed on the deck jumped into the sea.

Herman said, 'I have not enjoyed such a day since we went after the wild boar in the forest at home.'

That evening the fog rolled away and the fleet came together.

The skipper of the Francia made a report to the captain of the fleet, naming this sailor and that soldier for outstanding bravery. The name of Herman was mentioned more than once.

The captain sent the skipper of Francia on to the colonel, Maximinius, to repeat his despatch.

The upshot was that Herman was enrolled as a soldier of Imperial Rome, and given a new-minted silver coin in token of the contract between himself and Caesar Augustus.

The heat increased.

The ships idled on the still hot sea that began to smell now like rotting figs.

VII

'I think,' said Phocas, 'we may be bound for the garrison in Egypt. Alas, it's too late for us to see the great queen. Cleopatra is dead.'

The ships anchored in the Nile delta.

Only the officers, military and marine, were allowed ashore. There would be no more desertions. The shadow of the enchanting queen still fell across the sands and bewildered men of all kinds and conditions.

Phocas told Herman about the Egyptian wars and the death of Cleopatra and Mark Anthony.

'She must have been a wonderful woman to look at,' said Herman.

'If she had been a fish-wife,' said Phocas, 'nobody would

have looked at her twice.'

They spent a hot summer month in that Egyptian harbourage, confined on ship-board.

At last, after many banquets ashore, captain and colonel were rowed from the palace steps in one small boat. They inclined their heads with utmost courtesy, talking and listening gravely. They had been reconciled in the general's tent. But still their faces were cold.

'We will not be joining the Egyptian garrison,' said Phocas.

VIII

Great ceremony on the waterfront at Joppa: beating drums, trumpets blowing, standards lifted high.

The columns embarked, bronze-gleaming in the hard light, boots throbbing on the cobbles: sergeants and centurion forming them into squares.

There the colonel, Maximinius, took a formal farewell of the captain of the ships – the hands raised in stiff salute, the faces carved out of stone.

Then a single trumpet call, thrilling. The three squares moved into columns and went, narrow crashing waves, through the squares and streets of the port – and on out into the desert.

They stopped under wayside palm trees to eat bread and dates and drink wine. A murmuration like a tree loaded with starlings went through the troops.

'This is the worst that could have happened,' said Phocas the Greek. 'A Parthian War. Blood in the sand. Broken swords beside a ford. Vultures.'

'I'm glad of that,' said Herman. 'I find I very much enjoy fighting.'

A trumpet blew. The columns reformed.

The march ended in Jerusalem, in the square before the villa of the Roman governor.

Maximinius was a week establishing his camp.

IX

There followed a time of interminable boredom.

After the daily parades, little to do but drink and dice-throwing.

The Jewish girls and the Greek girls covered their faces from the soldiers. The merchants and temple priests paid no attention to the foreigners.

The soldiers had to content themselves with the licensed houses.

The soldiers had strict orders to give no offence to the temple and the city and its people.

'The Jews are a deep and a subtle race,' said Phocas over the beer-mugs. 'Their curiosity of spirit can be called a God-seeking. They are forever searching out, with a kind of fearful joy, the nature and attributes of Jahwe the one God. One might call them fanatics of the absolute. They wait for a great leader, a Messiah, to free them of their oppressors.'

'We Germans have a score of gods,' said Herman. 'We will rot in this place. Let us have battles, and soon.'

'You'll get your blood and wounds soon enough,' said Phocas. 'Meantime we'd do well to drink our beer.'

Then Phocas told Herman about a prophecy of the Roman poet Virgil. 'He is not a great poet like our Homer, of course, but he is good considering that he comes from a nation of such power-mongers and bare-faced exploiters. Virgil has written about the imminent coming of a King of peace to the whole world. He is to be a child, that prince.'

'I hope,' said Herman, 'that it doesn't come too soon, the

pax mundi. Otherwise we lose our occupations. That would be a pity. I long for battles and sieges. I take delight in war.'

X

They were called into line to smoke out a nest of young Jewish guerrillas, 'zealots,' who had been making raids on Roman outposts all that year.

The zealots hid out in caves in the mountains.

One column marched north.

'There'll be no fighting,' said Phocas. 'They have spies everywhere. They'll melt from us like smoke.'

'I hope not,' said Herman. 'My sword is crying out for blood.'

The zealots were in the caves, waiting for them. The caves were full of eyes. Then those eyes shone with light and laughter in the sun.

Before the soldiers could deploy, the zealots were on them like a wave.

The zealots broke on the bronze shields and swords. Not a man of the zealots fled. The last few of them stood waiting for death, laughing.

'They are a strange people,' said Phocas. 'I think they will do marvellous things in the world, the Jews.'

XI

There were no frontier wars. 'I have not known a winter of peace like this,' Maximinius the colonel said in the mess to his captains and commanders. 'I have had letters from Rome. The length and breadth of the empire, not one sword rises and falls.'

In a corner of the soldiers' canteen, away from the banter and the bawdy choruses, a few of the soldiers discussed serious things over their beer.

21

They discussed death and what comes after death: Phocas and Herman and a sergeant from Brittany.

Herman said, 'In Germany we know what happens to good soldiers after they die in battle. Their souls go straight to the drinking-hall of the heroes, called Valhalla. There, at the long table, they drink and sing battle-choruses for ever. I can think of no better thing. I pray I won't live to be a foolish old man mumbling at the fireside, being fed with mash.'

The Breton sergeant said, 'We Celts have a legend of immortality too. Those who have lived their lives well set out at the time of death to an island in the far western ocean. There is music always, the trees are heavy with apples, there is neither slow withering nor onset of tempest. For the people of The-Land-of-the-Young it is always blossom time.'

'A handful of dust in a jar,' said Phocas.

XII

Towards midwinter, detachments from the company were sent here and there in Judaea, to keep the peace.

The senate in Rome was planning to levy a poll-tax. In order for a register to be compiled, every householder in the land was ordered to go to his own tribal town and make his declaration and mark at the office there.

As the 20 men of one detachment marched south from Jerusalem, a centurion explained the situation.

'Bethlehem,' he said, 'that's our place. I don't suppose you ever heard of it. Nor have I. A country village. Tame routine stuff. There's bound to be a few punch-ups, disturbances, over bargains and tribal affairs and women. If we're lucky, there might even be a small riot. It won't be longer than a week.'

The sergeant from Brittany, Phocas the Greek, and Herman were sent to the north gate.

From dawn onwards, 'the tribe of David' arrived, singly and in small groups – shepherds, quarrymen, farmers, fishermen, labourers, scriveners.

The three soldiers at the north gate let them through.

About noon Phocas said he was half choked with sand. The Breton said he would go for a drink too.

'We'll be back soon,' said Phocas.

Herman was left alone at the gate, burning.

The Jews came in, alone or in small groups, all through the afternoon.

From the village lanes and streets came scattered shouts and music.

After sunset, the Jews went to the inn, for soup and bread and cheese. The inn buzzed like a hive.

After sunset, it got cold. No more tax-payers stood outside the north gate, asking the soldier-on-guard to be let in.

Herman shivered under the stars. He was cold, hungry, and tired.

(When a boy in the Alps is set over the wolf-fires, he stays until he is relieved.)

A few hillmen came, one carrying a lamb. After them, there was only the darkness, the cold, and the stars.

Herman thought of the wine, brought up from the cold cellar below, and the hot loaves on the inn tables, and the goat cheese.

'What's keeping Phocas and the Frenchman?' he thought. But said nothing.

A few village youths mocked Herman. One threw a stone. The youths passed on, laughing, among the shadows.

From the inn, the choruses got more raucous. There were shouts of anger, and pleas from the inn-keeper, and rallies of laughter.

23

It was to be a long night of revelry in Bethlehem.

At midnight Herman heard a stirring in the sand.

Three shadows: a man, and a girl on donkey-back, smelling of wind and stars.

'I'll light a lantern,' said Herman. 'Wait.'

So Herman lit a lantern at the north gate.

The man and the girl on donkey-back passed through, into the midnight village dappled with candle-flames and lamp-flames, and so on along the noisy street towards the inn.

Still the soldier stood.

A Christmas Exile

That winter – I remember it too well – my mother took ill suddenly. An ambulance arrived one morning and took her to the infirmary.

It was more than my poor father, the brewery worker, could handle: three children! I was told that same afternoon: 'You're to go for a week or two to your granny's in Orkney till your mother's better. Your case is ready and packed. The 'St Rognvald' leaves Leith at five o'clock.'

'But the school,' I said. 'The school play! We start rehearsals tomorrow morning. I'm the third king.'

'It can't be helped,' said my harassed father. 'There'll be another boy to take your place. I've sent a note to the headmaster. Put that thick muffler round your neck.'

'But Christmas,' I said. 'Surely I'll be home for Christmas?'

'Of course you will. Your mother'll be much better soon. Hurry up now. We have to catch that bus down to Leith.'

Three women in the landing were whispering, 'Complications … miscarriage … serious. …' And they looked at me sorrowfully.

Scarfed, bonneted, overcoated, I followed my father down the steps of our Marchmont tenement.

My father was carrying my cheap pasteboard suitcase. At the outer door I met Tommy Macnamara, my chum.

'Where do you think you're going?' said Tommy, wide-eyed, 'Miss Letham was wondering why you weren't at the school.'

'Get out of my way,' I said. 'I'm going for a holiday to the Orkneys.'

Tommy gaped at me, in awe and envy.

'Hurry up!' cried my father from the darkling pavement outside. 'Here it comes, the bus.'

When the boat left Leith, at 5 o'clock, it was dark, and the port was a great cluster of lights. Beyond that, Edinburgh would be a near-infinite maze of lights, an intricate many-coloured web reaching out to Juniper Green and Silverknowes and Duddingston and the Pentlands.

Somewhere, lost in that jewellery of night, was the one muted hospital glow where my mother lay, thin and fevered.

The wind swooped and keened along the Forth waters as the 'St Rognvald' left the quay. The ship was awake, her heart beating as she made for the North Sea.

'It'll be a dirty night,' said the white-coated steward to one of the crew.

Then he caught sight of me, the sole passenger except for a commercial traveller. And he said kindly, 'What's your name?'

'Ken,' I said.

'Well, Ken,' said he, 'the wind's in the north-east, and if I was you I'd go and lie down in your bunk. It's going to be choppy. We don't want you being sick, eh?'

'I'd rather be on deck,' said I. 'I'm a good sailor. I'm never sick.'

(I had travelled this way before, many a time, in high summer, when the sea is brimming and large and full of songs, and midnight a glimmer in the north).

The red-nosed commercial traveller asked, for the third time, when was the bar going to open ....

'When I'm ready,' said the steward, who obviously knew the man of an old date and wasn't too impressed by him.

Once out into the North Sea and headed for the Pole Star, the half-gale struck the ship and she began to roll mightily. In the darkness I (leaning over the rail) could see the white crests of the waves. A wilderness of wild dark horses was streaming past us! And the wind howled in the rigging.

The sea had never behaved this way before, in my minding. I felt excited leaning over the great black sounding heave.

But soon I felt the cold in bones and head and stomach. It was time to seek out my bunk. I had, to get to bed, to pass the bar. And there the commercial traveller swayed, his nose redder than ever, and communed with his glass of whisky the way a fortune-teller gazes into a crystal ball bemused and all-knowing. He gave me a bleary wink as I passed.

Rocked in the cradle of the deep, my Aunty Mabel used to sing that ballad, contralto, at soirees and family gatherings. The ship bucked and lurched and swooned through black troughs of sea, as I lay in my bunk; and the tumult soothed me to sleep at last....

I had never stayed at my granny's croft in winter.

How different everything was, compared to the bright days of summer! The kind old lady lit the Tilley lamp at three o'clock in the afternoon, and she crammed the glowing stove with peats that had been cut and carted home from the hill last summer. (I had been one of the peat-spreaders.)

Instead of the long lingering summer light, the sky was crammed with stars. I looked from the door in amazement one night at the swishing swirling silk skirts of the Northern Lights over the hill.

She was good to me, my granny.

When I came home from the shore, day after day, a smoking bowl of Scotch broth was set before me. And afterwards, her own cheese and her own oat-cakes. They seemed to taste of the lush summer grass and the field surging with corn.

Then she would light her hissing Tilley lamp.

We sat, till nine or ten o'clock, at each side of the glowing stove that burbled now and then with little yellow spurts of flame, and sometimes sent a plume of steam out of the snorting kettle.

There were few books in the house, but that mattered nothing. My granny's mouth was full of old stories: witches, the press-gang, shipwrecks, smugglers, lairds and ministers and ghosts and tinkers.

Shame on me, for the first week I enjoyed my solitary comings and goings so much, by the shore and sheep-paths and village, that I had few thoughts to spare for my poor sick mother, or for Tommy Macnamara and my brothers and sister, or for the douce canny citizens of Marchmont.

One afternoon, as I stood in the doorway watching the early sunset (it was like the blacksmith's forge in the village, all crimson and jet), there came loitering out of the twilight a solitary snowflake. It lit on my hand and lay there, exquisite winter jewellery; soon my young blood melted it.

'Come in for thee broth,' urged my granny.

That solitary snowflake was the herald of millions and trillions.

While I slept that night, the wind got up and stuffed and quilted the island with immensities of snow.

It was thrilling, eating duck eggs and oatcakes at breakfast time, to see through the window the island transfigured by that dazzling robe of snow! Fencing posts were half-buried, sheep cried from a lee wall, a dog barked thin and cold from a distant farm. An abandoned car nuzzled a white drift. Timmy the beachcomber stood, a black exclamation mark, between the boatshed and the beach. The island was all crystal and swansdown.

'There's more snow coming,' said my granny. 'Mark my words.'

After that first enchanted morning, a great dark blizzard moved in from the north and buried the island. It went on and on for two days and nights. To go outside for peats or eggs was to become a ghost. The north wind howled in the chimney. Except for the merry crackling of the fire, the only sound was the incessant hush-hush-hushing of snow; and the bleak words I spoke to the old woman, and her wise kind words to me. 'It'll soon be over,' she said. 'I've seen worse snow than this, many a time.'

During the second day of the blizzard, I began to think longingly of home. The wireless said there was snow further south too, in the Grampians and the Lothians and the Borders.

I thought of Marchmont in the snow, and the Meadows black with students coming and going with their books. I thought of the school, and our class-room where they would now be well into rehearsals for the Nativity play. (Who would have taken my place as the Third King?) I thought of Princes Street, and the big shops blazing with coloured lights and tinsel; and, after dark, that entire magic glittering mile.

Boys and girls, men and women, would be going home, muffled and red-cheeked, their arms full of parcels! And a hundred commercial travellers went from pub to pub, no doubt, with scarlet noses.

Most of all (for some reason) I thought of the Royal Mile. The Castle and Holyrood had known a thousand or more echanted snowfalls. Did the tall tragic Queen of Scots catch her breath with wonderment some morning, looking over the immaculate fields to Arthur's Seat? I thought of St Giles' echoing with medieval carols. John Knox – did he have a plum dumpling in his house on Christmas Day; or was the season all flummery and foolery to that stern man? There was the tombstone that the poet Burns had had set up in the Canongate Kirkyard for the poet Fergusson: that stone would be wearing a white bonnet on a day like this.

I thought of a sick woman in a hospital bed; perhaps she was beyond kenning of Christmas, and of kings and a cold cowshed under an inn.

The blizzard had blown itself out on the third morning. There was a patch of cold blue sky over the hill.

I went outside after breakfast to hide my misery and desolation and home-sickness.

'This'll never do,' I said to myself, wiping tears from my face with a grey mitten.

For there, drawing to a halt on the Siberian road below, was the post van.

Albert the postman got out, whistling. His cheeks were two apples. He came lurching up the path to the croft of Smelt with a parcel and a letter.

'You look that lonely. Why don't you build a snowman for a chum?' said Albert to me, and put the letter into my hand. He set the parcel inside the door. 'Stops thu, boy, and tak a dram!' cried granny.

While they discussed what havoc the blizzard had wrought – sheep buried, a boat ashore, a child born suddenly in such-and-such a croft without benefit of doctor or nurse, the silvery breath of an old fisherman shorn – I opened my letter. It was a card with a picture of a stage-coach and a log-fire: Happy Christmas from Tommy.

Albert licked the last amber drop from his whisker and went

and started up his red van. (The snow ploughs had been at work on the island roads since early morning.)

Granny called from inside, 'The parcel – it's from your father. So kind of him. A box of groceries. What kind of stuff's this? – crystallised fruit, jellied eels in a jar, Brazilian coffee beans! ... And there's a letter, too!'

She put on her silver spectacles. 'Oh, good news!' she cried.

'Your mother's home! And she's much better! ... And you, Ken, you're bidden to take the south boat from Kirkwall on Monday afternoon. You'll be home on Christmas Eve.'

More and more blue patches appeared in the sky. The islands lay around like white whales. The sun came out – the sea-road all the way from Orkney to Leith would be a blue-and-silver dazzle!

From inside the Leith taxi, I could see people coming singly and in small groups through the snow to the lighted church. It was almost midnight. The taxi stopped at traffic lights. My father, leaning forward, was deep in some good-natured wrangle with the taxi-man.

I got out, unobserved. I crunched and slithered through the snow towards the candles, the crib and the first carol.

The congregation were all strangers to me. But I could imagine my granny kneeling, and the red-nosed commercial traveller, and my mother, and Tommy Macnamara, and the island postman, and Timmy the beachcomber, and all the poor and lost and lonely folk of the earth.

Soon the mystery would be shown forth.

I went among them. I knelt down.

Anna's Boy

There was a child, a boy, up at the croft of Auding; everybody knew that, but nobody in the island had seen him. Not once.

Nell the howdie wife had seen him, the day he was born four years ago, but Nell was in the kirkyard two winters now.

Anna the mother was strange. Nobody crossed her threshold, neither neighbour nor the cousin from the far end of the island, he that had the big farm and might have been glad to help her and the child; if not with money, then with eggs, butter, tatties and smoked bacon. She wanted nothing to do with him and his charity.

Sometimes an inquisitive soul would make an attempt to see the child. Anna couldn't stay indoors always. She had to go sometimes to see to her two sheep, and to the grocery van that stopped at the end of the road every Friday morning.

Three times Bella Scad tried to get into the house to see the child, when Anna was at field or well or van. And three times the door was locked! A door locked! – such a thing had never been known in the island before. The queer lass had turned the key in the lock and put it in her apron pocket before leaving the house.

Bella Scad pressed her face against the pane. There was no sign of the bairn inside: her eyes saw nothing but the interior of a very poor house, without a single ornament on the mantelpiece or a picture on the wall. All the needful things were there, girnal and lamp and spinning-wheel and kettle and pot and a little fire of peats blinking on the hearth. But no child – there was no boy to be seen or heard. As Bella Scad squashed her face still harder against the pane, a cold voice behind her said, 'Are you wanting something?'

It was Anna, come back from the grocery van too soon with her few messages.

For once in her life the gossip and tale-bearer was lost for words. 'I was just wondering . . . if thu were all right . . . for I havena seen thee for a day or two . . .'

'When I need you,' said Anna, 'I'll send for you.'

And with that Bella Scad slunk off like a chidden dog, and Anna turned the key in her door and went inside.

Of course, there were all sorts of rumours about the boy. He was mis-shapen, he was an idiot, he was blind, he was a deaf-mute. For one or other of those reasons Anna didn't let the boy over the door. There was one very wicked old man who lived on the far side of the hill. 'He's maybe dead,' said this cruel old creature one winter night in the smithy, 'and buried in the peatmoss.'

The men who gathered for news and discussion in the smithy every evening were so shocked that there was silence for a while. Then Thomasina Brett the blacksmith's wife cried from the door between smithy and house, 'I heard a bairn's voice from Anna's place no later than yesterday, when I was going down to the shore. Shame on you!'

The smithy debaters turned black looks on the wicked old man. And he slunk away into the night, and never came back for a month.

Bridie the tinker lass said she had seen the boy, one day when Anna was at the well with her bucket. The door stood open – Bridie had gone in. 'He was more like an angel than a bairn,' said Bridie. (But Bridie was forever seeing ghosts, trows, mermaids.)

Still there was much talk in the village and in the farms about Anna and her child that no one had ever clapped eyes on.

'I tell you what,' said Roberta Manson at the W R I meeting, when the ladies were nibbling their dainties and sipping their tea, 'once Anna's boy turns five, he'll have to come out and be seen. The law of the land says every child must go to school at the age of five' . . . The island ladies nodded sagely over the tea-cups. Anna wouldn't be able to hide her bairn away for ever. One day next August the boy would have to go to the village school with his satchel under his arm.

* * *

But Anna's boy did not go to school next August, among the little flock of new 'scholars,' boys and girls, all mute with the wonderment of blackboard, slate pencils, coloured chalks, wall-charts, map of the whole world, and Miss Carmichael who was both kind and severe.

Anna's boy was where he had always been, at home.

Of course enquiries were made. The school attendance officer knocked at Anna's door, and got no reply. He pressed the sneck – the door was locked. Mr Smith the general merchant who was the island representative on the education committee called. The door opened. Anna's cold face looked into his. No, said she, the bairn wouldn't be going to the school. If Mr Smith wanted more information, let him ask Dr Fergusson. Smith the grocer tried to look over Anna's shoulder. There was no boy to be seen. But over the mantelpiece a picture was pinned – a crude child's picture, in coloured crayons, of a flower, but such a flower as Mr Smith had never seen in Orkney or in any place he had visited, ever. The flower enriched the poor room.

Then Mr Smith found himself standing outside in the cold. For Anna had shut the door against him.

* * *

'Oh yes,' said Dr Fergusson to Smith the merchant, 'I've seen the boy – of course I've seen him. He's a delicate child. No point in him going to school now that winter's setting in. Never be able to trudge through snow, in the teeth of gales. Impossible. Maybe in spring, at daffodil time, he could give the school a try, to see how things go then.' Yes, by all means Dr Fergusson would write out a certificate . . .

So, it seemed the appearance of Anna's boy would be postponed for a while yet.

* * *

Two days before Christmas there was a school party. What excitement! The severe schoolroom was suddenly an enchanted cavern, hung with decorations and murals the children had made themselves. The desk had been pushed into a corner to make way for a long trestle, and it was loaded with sandwiches, cakes with icing and marzipan and spice and sultanas, and with pyramids of oranges and apples, and ranked bottles of lemonade. And there was a Christmas tree that glittered with coloured lights: the first illuminated Christmas tree ever seen in the island (for electric power had only come the previous autumn).

And the twenty school-children were there in their best suits and dresses, and they made as much noise as any crowd at the Lammas Fair; except that their cries were purer and sweeter. And, on this evening, Miss Carmichael made no attempt to restrain them.

Outside, a wind from the Atlantic howled about the school, and from time to time showers of hail crashed against the tall school windows.

But the storm served only to increase the merriment inside.

Until, suddenly, the whole school went dark! The babble ceased abruptly. A small girl began to cry. There were other whimpers here and there.

'It's all right,' said the voice of Miss Carmichael out of the darkness. 'It's just a power cut. The lights will come on again. Find your desks and sit down. It looks as if I'll have to go into the school-house and look for our old paraffin lamps. I hope I can find them. I hope there's some paraffin in the cupboard' . . .

But Miss Carmichael didn't sound any too sure; and there was a fresh outburst of sobs and wails from some of the shadowy pupils groping among the hard shadows of desks.

The outer door opened. A butterfly of light entered, and went wavering down the corridor between the rows of desks. Then it was petals, a folded flower of light. It lingered beside the Christmas tree, and hung over it at last, steadfast and tranquil, a star.

Miss Carmichael and the twenty glimmering pupils were silent.

'I'm Anna's boy,' said the stranger who had carried the lighted candle through the storm.

Miss Tait and Tommy and
the Carol Singers

There was a very severe old lady called Miss Tait who lived alone with her cat Tompkins in a big house at the end of the village.

All the village children avoided Miss Tait's house. She was especially severe if they came round on Bonfire Night, or to collect for charity – though it was well known that Miss Tait was the richest person in the island, by far. The tin tea caddies on her mantelpiece, it was said, were stuffed with musty-smelling moth-eaten twenty-pound notes. They put treacle on her door-knob at Halloween, and once they tied an empty tin to the tail of Tompkins the cat.

How enraged Miss Tait was! She phoned the island councillor, district councillor, J.P., and the police office in Kirkwall. But nobody could find out who the wicked young scoundrels were who had inflicted such mischief on Miss Tait and Tompkins.

Miss Tait found her grandfather's thick hickory stick in the attic, and blew the cobwebs off it. 'This,' said Miss Tait to Tompkins, 'is for the next young villain who comes round this house!'

And she made a fierce flourish with the stick until it whistled through the cold grey air of her kitchen.

Tompkins took one alarmed leap from floor to dresser-top.

The air was cold because it was mid-December and Miss Tait had lit no fire since the miners' strike began.

The village children practised their carols, to sing here and there about the island two nights before Christmas.

All the children except Tommy practised their five or six chosen carols round the school piano, after four o'clock.

Tommy was not included because he had a voice like a crow; and, more than that, whenever the children did anything communally like a play or a bonfire, Tommy always ruined it with some piece of stupidity or clumsiness.

Two nights before Christmas, the choir, well muffled in bonnets and mittens and scarves, set out in lightly falling snow to sing their carols. How pure and sweet their voices sounded outside the inn, and at the teacher's house and the manse and the doctors' house – *Once in Royal David's City, Away in a Manger, O Come All Ye Faithful.*

As the choristers went through the falling snow to sing at their last station, the block of new council houses, one of them wondered where Tommy might be?

'Oh,' said Mary who had the sweetest voice in the choir, 'I saw him down at the shore, with a sack, just at sunset.'

After they had sung *Mary's Boy* outside the council houses – and got more 5p and 10p pieces, so that the collecting box rang like a bell – Willie (who was game for anything) said, 'Let's go and see what kind of a Christmas Miss Tait is having' . . .

That caused a fluttering among the girls! They had heard about Miss Tait's stick and how she meant to thwack boys and girls who came about her doors.

'It'll be miserable in there!' said Sandra. 'No Christmas tree. No decorations. Not even a fire!'

But, greatly daring, softly through the snow they stepped to Miss Tait's window and peeked through. They nearly fell on top of each other in astonishment! For who was sitting in Miss Tait's armchair, eating an apple, but Tommy the outcast! And there was a fire of wood in the grate, burning bright! And there was a sack of wood – shore-gathered – on the floor. And every now and then Tommy threw a piece of a fish-box on to the flames. The bowl on the sideboard was heaped with apples, grapes, oranges, bananas and nuts.

Miss Tait looked *very* happy, sitting in her rocker.

But suddenly she was aware of the faces at the window. She made towards the door. And the silent choristers, clustered outside the window, fled. The girls shrieked! Mary slipped in the snow, and cried in terror.

'Come back!' cried Miss Tait from the open door, and it was as if her voice glowed like a candle and trembled like a bell, through the falling snow, 'I have *a new pound coin* for each of you.'

The choristers returned one by one, with smoking breaths. They stood outside Miss Tait's open door. They sang, *We Three Kings of Orient Are*.

Then one by one they came in and stood by the fire. 'Tommy brought me driftwood,' said Miss Tait. 'Now, who likes oranges?'

Tompkins purred merrily beside the blaze.

39

A Christmas Story

Rolf Scroogeson was the meanest man in Orkney. If somebody sent him a Christmas card, he would say 'Bah!' and throw it in the fire. Then he would quickly retrieve it, all scorched and smoky as it was – for it might come handy to write a note on.

His fire was two peats that licked each other half-heartedly with small red tongues. That fire would not have kept a cat warm.

A peedie boy stood in the snow and called, 'A Merry Christmas, Mr Scroogeson, when it comes.'.. Rolf Scroogeson put such a blue cold look on the boy that might have stricken him on the spot, there and then, but the boy ran red-cheeked through the fields to share his winter merriment with farms and crofts near and far.

Rolf Scroogeson looked into his wretchedly bare cupboard and saw that he had only a crust left and half-a-spoon of tea and no sugar. Grumbling about the expense of everything, he set out in the late afternoon to the village shop. It was Christmas Eve.

He saw a snowman in a field smoking a cold pipe upside-down. Rolf was so mean he stole the pipe from the snowman's mouth and put it in his pocket.

'Merry Christmas,' said Bella Muir who kept the village shop. . . . 'Your goods get dearer and dearer,' was all the reply she got, plus a barbed look. A blizzard came on as Mr Scroogeson walked home with his few errands. The snow came thicker and faster, it whirled round and round, a dense ravelment and confused Rolf Scroogeson entirely.

At last he saw a wall and a spectral building, and was glad, because the drifting snow had half-choked him. He would shelter here till the storm passed. He went through a gate.

He discovered, to his surprise, that he was in the kirkyard. He crouched down behind a stone. The blizzard lasted a long time. Also the darkness was coming down. Rolf snoozed for a time. Then, when he woke up, the snowstorm had passed. The moon shone on the white-heaped kirkyard. The moon lay bright on the tombstone in front of Rolf Scroogeson. He read: ROLF SCROOGESON on the cracked neglected face of the stone.

* * *

We all know the rest of the story: how he went home and opened the kist under his bed and brought out heaps of mouldy ten-pound notes and little tarnished tinkling rivers of sovereigns. And how he distributed that hoard to all the poor and infirm of the island. And how he greeted the red-faced peedie boy next morning and gave him 50p; so that in utter surprise, the peedie boy fell into a snowdrift.

And how Rolf passed away at last, a merry old man full of years and friendship, and lies in the summertime kirkyard.

The Box of Fish

They had had a good catch of haddocks in the afternoon. Now it was evening. In the tarred shed above the shore the four fishermen were sitting round the cold bogeystove. The oldest one kneaded the blue back of his hand with urgent knuckles.

They had not gone home after mooring the Sea Quest and landing the boxes of fish. Instead they had sent the boy up to the hotel for a bottle of rum on tick.

They could see the whirls of snow through the window of the shed.

'We just got in in time,' said Alex. He dropped a lighted match upon the driftwood and coal and paraffin in the bogey. It roared into flame at once.

'We'll just have one dram,' said The Partan. 'Then home for tea. The wife'll be wondering.'

The boy came in out of the darkness, empty-handed.

'Mr Blanding said, 'No cash, no rum,"' said the boy. "Tell them that,' said Mr Blanding. 'There's more than ten pounds against The Partan on the slate,' he said.'

They spent more than five minutes discussing the hotelier's

character in the blackest of terms.

'You see them boxes of fish,' said Tim Smith to the boy. 'Tell him, a box of haddocks for a half-bottle rum.'

The boy took the box of fish in both hands and staggered out with it into the darkness.

A quarter of an hour later he was back with a half-bottle of rum.

'There's cups in the cupboard,' said a man with a black beard, Dave the skipper.

The boy brought over cups, darkly stained with ancient tea, and gave one each to the four fishermen round the bogey stove.

'What did you see in the village?' said The Partan to the boy. 'Did you see Mary-Ann looking for me?'

'No, I didn't,' said the boy.

Dave the skipper gravely dropped four musical measures of rum into the cups, one after the other. Rich Caribbean fragrances mingled with the smells of salt and tar.

'I saw two strangers,' said the boy. 'They were looking for a place for the night. They didn't look to me as if they could afford the hotel.'

Alex smacked his lips. 'There's worse things,' he said, 'than a drop of rum on a winter night.'

Tim set down his empty cup on the floor.

'Go and tell Mary-Ann,' said The Partan to the boy, 'I'll be home in ten minutes. Tell her we had a good catch.'

The boy went out into the night. It had stopped snowing. The sky had cleared. In at the open door stars throbbed cold and brilliant.

* * *

The boy was back in five minutes. Mary-Ann had told him to inform James (The Partan) that she didn't care when he came home, if ever. His tea was spoiled anyway. She would rather have the house to herself than have a poor thing of a drunk man snoring in the armchair beside the fire. She was in no hurry to see him. She had this Yule cake to bake. He would just be in the way.

The empty half-bottle lay on the floor.

The skipper laughed. 'Well,' he said, 'there's no hurry in that case. We deserve a drink. We've had a cold hard day of it.'

Three heads nodded about the ruddy stove.

The boy said he had glimpsed the two strangers between the Store and the kirk. They still didn't seem to have found a place.

'Boy,' said the skipper. 'You see that box of fish against the wall. Take it up to the hotel. Mr Blanding will give you a half-bottle of rum for it. Hurry now.'

The top half of the bogey was red-hot. At the dark window snowflakes whirled and drifted, a horde of gray moths.

Alex licked the last drop of rum from his moustache.

* * *

At the end of half an hour the boy had still not returned.

'What can be keeping him?' said The Partan.

'Maybe Blanding wouldn't deal with him,' said Tim. 'Maybe Blanding thinks he's got enough fish for one night.'

They waited another ten minutes. Nobody spoke.

'What I'm feared of,' said Dave, 'is that he might have gone over the pier in the blizzard.'

They waited till the thick-falling snow had dwindled to a few gray loiterers under the star-flung sky; then they put on their bonnets and oilskins and blew out the lamp. It was all right – there were still five boxes of fish at the wall. They went, one after the other, up the stone steps to the village street.

At the hotel Mr Blanding said no, he hadn't seen the boy

since the rum-fish transaction earlier in the evening.

The four fishermen went and stood at the edge of the pier, looking down. It was ebb-tide. They saw no broken body on the stones surrounded by a silver scattering of fish.

They trooped to the boy's house. The mother opened the door to them. 'You don't need to worry,' she said. 'Sam's done exactly what you told him to do. Old Ezra's had his fish, and blind Annie, and that cripple boy at the end of the village. Who else? Sam's been at a dozen poor doors – the ones you told him to go to. At the end of it he had two fish left. He told me about the hippies or beatniks or whatever you call them – he's out now looking for them.'

'That's all right,' said the skipper. 'We were just wondering.'

Sam's mother invited them in for a drop of something, seeing it was Yule time. But they said they'd better be getting home. There was another blizzard building up in the north.

The Christmas Dove

The rich merchant had a house on the hill outside the town. Servants came and went in the rooms, and tended the stable and garden and wells.

The merchant's children fed a dove in a golden cage, on cake and sweetmeats.

One day the smallest child left the cage door open, and the bird was up and away into the wind and sun. A servant tried to catch it, but it flew from his fingers and the servant measured his length in the dust.

Tearfully the children trooped into their father's office, to tell him about the lost dove.

'Tut-tut,' said he. 'Go away – I'm busy. Can't you see the clerks writing in the account books – a camel train leaves for Syria tomorrow. I've told you a hundred times not to come to the office during business hours . . . Sammy, tears is it? Why are you crying? The dove flown away – is that all? I'll buy three doves at the market tomorrow. Now go and leave us to get on with our work . . . Sixty bales of wool. A hundred jars of best oil . . .'

The merchant's children came out into the yard with dark stains on their faces.

There they saw a servant who was dust from head to foot, and with scratches on his arms. (This was the servant who had tried to catch the dove.) The children pointed at him. They laughed.

The dove was frightened. It had lived its whole life in the cage, from the time of the breaking of the egg, and the yellow wind and the stone alleys and the people coming and going in the village frightened it. The town birds darted at it. One bird cried: 'What are you, fluttering stranger?' And another with dusty wings said: 'Fly away, you milksop, there's little enough bread and seeds in this town . . .' A red bird screamed: 'Look out for the hawk! He lives up there, high, in his crystal cage of wind.'

Dearly the dove would have loved to be back in his safe golden cage in the merchant's villa, with children feeding him cherries and sweet crusts. But he did not know the way.

The dove flew out of the town, with its noise, dust and hostility. He darted over the desert sand, blown into undulations by the wind, with its palm trees and oases of water, and the golden eye of the sun above. Suddenly the sun was fractured, a wavering shadow covered the dove, and when he looked up what he saw was the yellow eye of the hawk.

The dove almost fell from the air, he was so frightened! But he gathered what wits and courage he had left, and he turned and flew towards a little green hill with sheep grazing on it, and a shepherd boy with a long crook. The dove fell panting on a stone. The sheep looked at him mildly. The boy broke off a piece of his loaf and offered it to him. Then the boy went down to the stream with a cup and filled it for the lost bird. The dove had never tasted anything as delicious as the oaten crust and the broken circles in the cup of water.

When the dove looked up, he could see the hawk going in a slow dark wheel northwards, after other prey.

47

'What's that boy up to now?' he heard a dark grumbling voice say. 'Look, boy, we don't keep you to feed a useless bird, we keep you to see that the sheep are safe. There's a ewe over there that's put her hoof in a bunch of thistles. See to it . . .'

Three shepherds came up from the village, each with a skin of wine, and all they did was complain about the village inn and the hordes of strangers in the village, and how the innkeeper was taking advantage of the situation to put up the price of his wine again. 'The scoundrel!' . . . 'An outrage.'

The boy ran to take the prickles out of the ewe's leg. The dove, frightened by the shepherds, unfurled his grey pinions to fly away. 'A good sign, a dove,' said one of the shepherds. 'It's usually that hawk after a new lamb.'

The dove scattered grey blessings on the sheep-fold, and flew south, away from the vigilant hawk. Now the sun had moved down the sky, and as it touched the horizon a flush engulfed the desert. Through an air red as wine the dove spied, far below, three travellers with laden camels. The travellers halted. They unburdened the camels and tethered them. They lit a fire under a rock. One opened a bag and passed food – oranges and cakes – to his companions. A silver wine flask shone in the firelight, passing from hand to hand, from mouth to mouth.

This too was a scene of peace. The dove trembled in the darkening air, then faltered and fell on the rock near the little tableau of travellers and animals, fire and refreshment.

'A dove!' cried one of the men. 'When it hung up there trembling, I thought it was our sign again.'

'Welcome, bird of peace,' said a deep gentle black voice. He offered a date to the dove. The dove took it into his beak.

'Fly away, dove,' said the third man. 'The desert is a dangerous place for you to be. Aren't you afraid of the hawk? There'll be nothing left of you after sunrise if you don't find a lodging, nothing but a few bones in the sand.'

'The whole world is a dangerous place,' said the traveller whose voice was like a golden harp. 'The meaning of history will be Death, all time will be a scattering of bones, unless we find the place soon.'

The dove flew higher and higher up among the stars. He hung there, trembling, uncertain which way to turn. Then, over the desert, he saw far away the lights of the little town. That was where he belonged. There were the children and the golden cage and the circles of cake and milk and safety.

But where, in all that hundred houses great and small, was the house he belonged to?

The dove hovered over the darkling town, with its watchman's lantern at the main gate, and the lamps burning in prosperous windows, and candles in poor men's niches.

The dove was as lost as he had been all day. (And somewhere the hawk sat furled, nourishing himself with dreams of blood and death.)

The dove, stooping lower, saw a friend! The shepherd boy, with a small lamb in his arms, had entered the town gate and now had set his face to the darkest part of the town. The dove hovered above the boy and the lamb. 'I'll come to no harm,' said the dove to himself, 'if I stay near this boy.'

The boy stooped in at a dark door, where there was only a glim of light. Shadowy animals moved about inside. It was (thought the dove) the poorest house in the town. A tall shadow, a man, bent over a kneeling shadow that held a bundle in her arms.

The shepherd boy stood in the doorway, afraid to go in.

But the dove flew on to the boy's shoulder, and paused there a moment, and flew up to a cold rafter, and furled there, under the stars.

The Poor Man in his Castle

A Christmas Story

I

When I got home to the island in mid-winter, Willie the handyman was waiting at the pier with the horse-and-trap.

'*A poor bleak house,*' said Willie, who is no respecter of the gentry, as the horse trotted and slithered up the wet track to the Hall. '*A sad place since your mother died, poor soul, in the summer.*'

As we got near the Hall, I could see that there was only one light, in the library. Every Christmas up to now, the house had been festive with lights.

My father met me at the library door. '*Welcome home,*' he said in a voice like pewter. '*I forgot you were coming today. Willie, light a fire in James's room . . . There might be something left in the stew-pot. Have a look. I know there's some cheese. I opened a bottle of wine in November when the laird of Norday was here. You could finish that off for supper . . .*'

My father looked old and ill.

He had been working for years on a study of the flowers and plants of the island.

'*How is the magnum opus going?*' I said.

'*It limps along,*' he said. '*I do what I can. If I have three more years, I can write 'finis,' and then I'll be glad to be rid of all this . . .*' And he made a little gesture with his hand, as if to dismiss the Hall and the manuscripts on his desk, and the islands and the great globe itself, and the host of winter stars.

'*Will I light the tree in the drawing room window?*' I said.

(Six years before, my mother had brought from Inverness the latest Christmas fashion, a tree with lighted candles. Prince Albert had introduced the vogue.)

'*Do what you like,*' said my father. '*Do what you like. For all the good it will do . . .*'

My father was a relic of the eighteenth century, distrustful of symbolism and the unrestrained imagination. Had not imagination ruined some of the great minds of his time – Swift, Blake, Cowper – and plunged others into wasteful melancholy, even the great Samuel Johnson . . .? The light of rationalism was enough for any intelligent man.

* * *

He had books of Hume and Voltaire sent to him, as soon as they were published, from the bookseller in Edinburgh. In religion he was nominally an Episcopalian, and he was civil enough to the rector who visited occasionally from Kirkwall. But privately he was cold towards religion in all its forms. The Book of Common Prayer lay on the table of the room where his wife had died; that was the only concession he made.

Willie came down from lighting the fire in my room.

'*A cold dreich place,*' Willie said. '*A cold dreich place . . .*'

My father heard him but said nothing. Willie Riddoch is the only islander he treats familiarly. They had fished trout together in childhood. Willie had shown him the best trout lures, and how to handle a boat. They had lived always under the same roof, for Willie's father had been the gardener and general factotum at the Hall.

My father went back to the library.

'Ah well,' I said to Willie, *'there'll be plenty of dancing and music and drinking between now and Twelfth Night. I won't have to hang about in the big house here like a ghost . . .'*

'Listen to me carefully,' said Willie. *'Things have changed greatly in this island since you were last here. A new minister was appointed in the Spring, Reverend Cornelius Cameron, a firebrand new out of college. His name was proposed to your father. And he said 'Call anybody you like, for all the difference it will make . . .' '*

It seems, from what Willie went on to tell me, that the new minister had gone like a cleansing fire through the island. He had denounced from his pulpit, powerfully, such ancient practices as the midsummer fire on the hill top, at Johnsmas. He had heard that some islanders, when they were sick, still visited old chapel ruins and so-called holy wells, and left offerings there. Halloween was an abomination, and Cromwell and his puritans had been undoubtedly right to banish Christmas (or Yule, as the islanders called it). The twelve-day-long midwinter feast, with all its papish rituals that were enacted in every farm and croft in Orkney – let it be engulfed by the cleansing fire of the Word itself, lest a worse fire engulf the souls of the islanders after the brief misery of this life was over.

'Well,' said Willie, *'he's got most of them shivering with penitence and dread. You'd never believe such a change could come over folk in a short time . . .*

* * *

A few honest good folk are to be uprooted from the merry God-given feasts from the old times. The ministers up to now, most of them, would have a dram and a plate of roasted goose at Johnsmas and Yule. So the tenants come to me, bewildered. And I send them on to your father. And the poor man is so stricken with grief and loneliness and poring over old leaves and roots, he sends them away. 'It makes no difference. Don't bother me. If you find any Primula Scotica on the cliff edges next Spring, come and tell me at once. I'll make it worth your while . . . He's your minister now, I can't do a thing about it' . . .'

So Willie Scott told me.

The dogs began to howl outside. Willie went and opened the door.

By the light of the lantern in the hallway we could see a small boy holding a cod in his two hands.

'What do you want at this time of night?' said Willie in his rough voice.

'This fish is for Sir Jeremiah Woolcot,' said the boy, and offered it.

'Who are you?' said Willie. 'I haven't seen you in the island before. What croft do you come from?'

I brought a platter from the kitchen and the boy laid the big fish, sparkling with snowflakes, on it . . .

He was certainly a very beautiful child, with dark curls and sea-blue eyes: but poorly clad for such a bitter night.

'Did you steal this fish?' said Willie sternly. (Willie would have made a good magistrate.)

'No,' said the boy, and smiled in a way that half-melted Willie's sternness, even.

'Well,' said Willie, 'tell your father the fisherman, whoever he is, he'll be paid tomorrow. We don't do business, up here at the Hall, near midnight.'

By this time my father, having heard the voices in the lobby, came out of the library.

'*The fish is not for sale,*' said the boy. '*Sir Jeremiah, it's a gift for you.*'

'*I thank you,*' said my father. '*This is the best gift I've had for a very long time. Won't you come in to the fire? I could give you a cup of something hot, and a bite to eat.*'

But the boy had gone, vanished among the curtains of snow, as if he had never been.

But there it was, the splendid fish, on the plate.

'*Well,*' said my father, '*that's our Christmas dinner provided for!*' He looked at Willie and me, and his old face crinkled with laughter and wonderment.

II

I visited two or three of the farms and crofts where I had always been made welcome. It was always a joyous time among the country folk, Yule.

But this winter there was a solemnity and a restraint, though the people were courteous and welcoming to me, as always.

'*Mr Cameron,*' said one old man, '*tells us we have been observing pagan superstitions, especially at this time of year. We must rid ourselves of them from now on. Mr Cameron was very forthright in his sermon last Sabbath, on the subject of drink. It's true, there's more than the usual amount of ale drunk about Thomasmas and Yule, and whisky too, but we thought of music and the circling ale-tub as a kind of reward for all the summer's toil, and a kind of thanksgiving too. But it seems we have been greatly mistaken, and our fathers before us.*'

The two sons of the farm set their faces hard. I knew they would have their Yule whisky, in some barn here or there in the island. One of them said '*Hogmanay,*' as if that strange barbaric word opened a door into unrestrained licence. (Hogmanay falls a week later than Yule).

The women of the farm, old and young, went about their

tasks with remote silent faces. They always withdraw into themselves when the gentry come among them.

'*Meantime,*' said old Samuel of Eastquoy, '*you're welcome to this house. You could even have supper with us, but it's coarse fare to what you're used to at the Hall.*'

I ate with them, porridge and cheese and bannocks and ale, after the farmer had blessed the meal. I mentioned the boy who had brought the gift of a cod to my father. They must know the name of the boy. (Everyone in that small island is known).

I described the boy as best I could.

The women looked at each other, and each one shook her head. There was no small boy of that description in Norday.

'*Ah well,*' I said, '*we've to eat the boy's fish tomorrow, my father and I, for our Christmas dinner. There have been more lavish Christmas dinners up at the Hall in times past.*'

'*My respects to your father. He has had his sorrows lately,*' said the good man as he bade me goodnight at his door.

And the wife and the two daughters and the daughter-in-law inclined their heads with grave courtesy.

On the road home I met the new minister.

We exchanged courtesies. He seemed to me to be a pleasant young man, and certainly alert and intelligent.

'*My regards to your father. I would visit him, but I fear I might get a poor welcome. He shows – I'll put it mildly – a certain indifference to religion . . . When you inherit Mr Woolcot, I hope we may work together for the betterment of the community here.*'

I told him, under the brightest stars of the year, that my sympathies were with the ancient good men who had built the way-side chapels here in Norday, and lit their candles and sung their Masses, so that the poor folk of Norday would know that Christ had come among them in the bread and wine, at Christmas especially.

The young minister looked at me in such wonderment as if I had been a painted savage from Tahiti or Madagascar.

I did not tell him that I had been reading, with interest, some essays by an English clergyman called John Henry Newman, in my comfortable quarters in Charlotte Square, Edinburgh.

When I got home, I unearthed my mother's Christmas tree and lit more candles on the branches than it had ever borne before, and I drew back the curtains so that the whole island might see it.

III

I think what happened that night may have been a dream.

I heard, before midnight, a small knocking at the door.

My father was deep in his specimen folders of leaves and roots, and as he is more than a little deaf, he did not hear the summons.

The small boy stood there.

'I'll take you to a place,' he said.

We walked together through the dark island. It was a still evening. The stars were very bright.

We passed through the village, and left the smithy and the kirk and the inn behind, and the boat houses.

There was a light in a croft window here and there.

Now we had left the fertile part of the island, and were walking in the barren hilly end, with peat cuttings above and wet-lands below. We followed a narrow sheep path, I following the boy, towards the bird-haunted cliffs.

In this region, I know, there was a chapel, not so dilapidated as those nearer to the farms and the village, where they had used the old stones to make byres and styes. Only a few young men after gulls' eggs came near this place.

We struggled up the last slope, and there was the ruin

glimmering with candle flames.

'*Come,*' said the boy. But I held back among the shadows.

I could see, inside, a company of shawled women, old and young. They were laying what seemed to be gifts on a long worn stone; cloth from a loom, a jar of oil, a dish of salt, a spray of unthreshed corn, a small coin. The silent ceremony was laved in candle-light.

Then, as frequently happens in the north, a wind got up suddenly – a breeze that whipped my coat-tails about my knees and fluttered my hat.

But the candles continued to burn in tranquillity and peace.

I turned to speak to the boy, my guide. But he was no longer there.

Presently the women quenched the candles.

The cliff hollow was lit by a star or two.

The women passed me, on their way home and one muttered '*A good Yule to you, Master Woolcot.*' And another said '*The stones will be built up again.*' And another chanted, in a low voice, '*Mother of God, keep us always,*'

They passed me, shadow after shadow, into the midnight of Christmas.

IV

This dream that I had was thirty years ago.

My father is long dead, and so is Willie, and many of the islanders I knew in my youth.

I only live in the Hall at Norday for a month in the summer with a few friends, to fish and shoot.

All but a few rooms of the Hall are uninhabitable. After my death the house will quickly revert to rat and blackbird and thistle . . . Perhaps this is as it should be; for my ancestors usurped the island three centuries ago, and wrung the people dry with their exactions. But recent legislation will ensure that in the course of a generation or two tilth and pasture and fishing-grounds will revert to their true owners, the islanders of Norday.

The Rev Cornelius Cameron did not stay long. Such talents as his were called for in the bigger towns of Scotland.

The present minister comes out of an older mould. His greatest intellectual pleasure is to read Virgil and Horace, and he laces his sermons with quotations in the original Latin, which greatly mystifies his congregation; though they are fond of him and never tire of relating his eccentricities.

Last week he countenanced a dog fight in the kirk, in the middle of his sermon, saying – among the snarling and yelping – that he thought Dale, the dog of Quoy farm, would quell Laddie of Smolgar, he would lay odds on it . . . Then, when the dogs were ejected by the beadle, his learned sermon resumed.

The Rev Samuel McAlistair and I take a dram together now and again, either in the Manse or up at the Hall, and we lend each other books, and smoke our pipes, and play an occasional game of chess.

The fact that I am a Catholic gives him no disquiet. A fortnight ago Samuel assured me that the poet Virgil, in one of his pastorals, foretold the birth of Christ. He recited the Latin to me in a fine Scottish birr, between the whisky decanter and the peat-fire.

V

I have never gone back to the chapel at the end of the sheep-path: fearing that thirty stormy winters may have undone it utterly. If I mention the place to a farmer or a fisherman, they shake their heads.

Most of them don't know that such a place had ever been there.

VI

My shooting guests, all (like myself) Edinburgh lawyers, left this morning after a pleasant fortnight's sport, in late summer.

After I have settled some estate business – much shrunken since my great-grandfather's time – I will follow them, tomorrow morning, in the ferry from Hamnavoe.

Last night we ate every last scrap of food in the cupboard, and emptied the last bottle in the cellar.

VII

My family for generations had owned the entire island. At harvest, the people – men and women – came from every farm and croft to labour in the ripe fields – the home farm – that lay all round the Hall.

But now the islanders work the land themselves, and pay a statutory paltry rent; and soon the corn-fields and pastures will be theirs entirely. This government directive, though it has impoverished me, is a good enactment. The farmers and crofters and fishermen have a direct interest in the fields and seas they harvest. The hills and shores of my island have never looked so prosperous; the wretched patches of poverty and poor husbandry that my childhood was acquainted with have become, in recent years, spread coats of green and gold.

You cannot imagine how melancholy the Hall is, with nobody in it but myself. How will it be in a month's time, with only ghosts in the great rooms, and in the rose and herb garden that my mother cultivated so lovingly?

There is no point in keeping on a factor or gardener.

A caretaker visits occasionally in winter to see that the Hall is lockfast and storm-proof.

The harvesters were busy that last day in the barley fields all round the big house. The Hall lay like a great wrecked ship among jostling golden seas.

The scythe-men did not defer to me, as they would have done to my father and (even more) to my grandfather, that old stern Tory.

Some of the men even turned their backs on me. They were not beholden to me any longer.

The women would have stopped their work with small silent acknowledgements as I passed, and one or two of the older women did still, rising from their sheaf-binding to stand with hands together and small courtesies of the head.

But the younger women turned sun-looks on me, never pausing in their stook-building. *'This is our land,'* they seemed to be saying, *'this is our bread and ale for next winter . . .'* And they immediately bent to their work again, as I passed along the side of the hill.

But I refused to be crushed by them.

I saw that, group by group, they were stopping work to eat at noon.

Some of the women were bringing baskets and stone jars of ale and milk from the shade of a stook, and spreading a cloth at the edge of the field. Then out came bannocks and cheese and eggs and crabs, and pewter mugs. And the workers gathered round, sitting and squatting. One old farmer mumbled a grace.

Children came running from the far side of the field. *'Gingerbread!'* they were shouting in the wind. *'Don't eat all the gingerbread!'*

I said, pitching my voice cheerfully into the wind, *'There's not a bite to eat in my cupboard. That old wreck of a Hall, not a mouse would live in it! The like has never been. That's good oatcakes and cheese you have there.'*

Some of them let on not to hear me. The like had never been, indeed — the great granary and deep cupboards of the Hall empty, while they who had been oppressed and half starved for hundreds of years feasted in the sun and the wind.

WELL, IT IS WELL DONE! — I thought I could read that message in the dark half-averted faces of the men.

And the women wished I would go away and leave them in peace. It is their nature to be hospitable. Not a beggar goes empty from their doors.

One young woman was looking at me, and whispering to a small dark-haired boy. I remembered the woman's vivid face, from a long-past winter, among sea-noises and a candle-flame. But that was thirty years back.

The women put oatcakes and cheese and chicken on a plate, and gave it to the boy, and pointed to me.

The boy ran across the stubble with this food for the hungry laird, and it was the same boy who had brought the sea-streaming cod to my father one Christmas Eve long ago.

He had the dark curls, the sea-blue eyes, the reverence and recklessness of giving.

'*This bread is for you,*' said the boy. There was no mistaking the song of his words either, a scatter of small bell-sounds in the wind.

I ate with my islanders for the first and the last time.

But still there was this unseen distance between us that could never be crossed, except by the enchanting boy who stood there laughing between the mother and myself.

Stars

I

It had been a bright midwinter morning, but the crofter of Banks knew there would be snow before sunset.

He could smell snow in the wind.

He licked his crooked forefinger and held it up. Yes, what small wind there was had shifted a point to the north.

He was going to feed his ox in the byre. Tonight – seeing that it was Yule – he would feed extra hay and turnips to the ox by lantern-light. 'That is,' he said to his small grandson, 'if we aren't drifted in with snow, and then you'll have to beat a path through the blizzard yourself to the byre, because I'm an old man, boy, and I go no further than the peat fire on a winter night.'

He laughed. And the boy Finn laughed too. He had seen his grandfather among the golden stooks at harvest, the strongest scythe-man in the island.

A granite stone lay on the road in front of them. The boy kicked it with his boot. A star flashed from the stone, between the schist and the steel, and lingered, and died on the bright air.

II

Mr Lorne the schoolmaster walked among the standing stones. There was the *sun circle,* a wide ring of tall stones on the moor, between two lochs, and the *moon circle,* a smaller, more intimate group. Apart from those two henges, there were individual stones set here and there, apparently at random, at the end of a field, above a quarry, on the tip of the sea loch ... A field away was the green hump that had the tombs of the ancient dead inside it, a chamber hewn out of immense stones.

The setting sun on winter solstice illumined one grave through a long low passage, on these few darkest days of the year.

'What is the meaning of the stones?' Mr Lorne wondered. 'There must be some key to the mystery, that is not known to us any more. But to those vanished people, the stones were thirled intimately to sun and moon and stars. Is there a wisdom vanished from the earth? Is our life drained of an ancient precious meaning?'

Out there on the moor, Mr Lorne laughed to himself.

That was all nonsense. It was merely that we had rejected those worn-out clay lamps of superstition and were busy replacing them with the lamps of science and learning, all over the world. And he, Mr Alistair Lorne, was the bearer of the light of knowledge in this poor island of crofters and fishermen in the north.

Already, most of the island children could read and do their sums, and some of them were quite bright: for example, young Finn of Banks farm, something might be made of him, a clerk in Kirkwall maybe, an auctioneer, maybe even a pupil teacher – all in good time.

A few flakes of snow drifted past; one lighted coldly on Mr Lorne's lip and melted there at once, and was a drop of tasteless water.

'And yet,' said the school-master, 'that snowflake is a congregation — a little city — of crystal hexagons. Consider: this island buried under an infinity of sixes, each like a hidden star in the storm! ... Truly, the earth is full of most intriguing mysteries.'

Mr Lorne went on to wonder if the ancient stone-builders had considered the snow crystal in their pattern of star-drift and their underground labyrinth of the dead.

'But no!' he cried out. 'Impossible! We did not know about that treasury of crystal stars locked in snow until the seeking mind of man discovered the microscope ... '

A sixth and a seventh snowflake fell on Mr Lorne's spectacles and dimmed his seeing, somewhat.

III

Sando the beach-comber, came up shivering from the shore with a sack of driftwood and shells, and a bannock and a few eggs he had gotten from the good wife of Ingarth farm.

She had also given him a shilling, the way it was Christmas.

'Now Sando,' she said rather severely, 'that's to buy butter and Lipton's tea. You won't spend it in the inn, will you?'

The shilling shone like a star in his hand. He promised he wouldn't buy whisky with it. Whisky, he declared, was the very last thing he would buy with the shilling!

His hut was cold, out there on the north-facing headland, when finally he got there, after much lingering and looking and talking to a sheep here and a boy there and a gull on the rock.

Oh, it was *cold* in the hut, though the air outside was bright.

He made a fire of knotted, dried hay and a few crumbs of purloined peat and a careful placement of broken driftwood.

He struck a match with blue fingers.

The dry hay flared. The peat pieces gave out a few wisps of blue smoke, then the driftwood began to sputter and spit.

There is always an anxious two minutes, while the new born
lion cub in the hearth decides to become a lithe roaring lion
or to return after all, to the cold and silence from which it
emerged.

Another fragment of wood sputtered and spat. A bright star
rose from the salted wood and drifted in the draught from the
door, and died.

Then the complete fire sank in a few sighings and whisperings.

'The wood's too wet,' said Sando. 'I should have let it dry out
for a few days ... '

'Am I to die of cold?' he said. 'Would Mrs Ingason of Ingarth
farm want me to die of cold, especially on Yule eve?'

He felt the shilling in his pocket.

He set out to buy a hot toddy in the inn, to keep the star of
life alive in him.

On the way he passed young Finn of Banks.

'My grand-dad says there'll be a blizzard,' said the boy to the
beachcomber.

A few young men passed them, going to the inn.

IV

Finn the boy stood between the loch and the sea.

He was watching for his father to come in from the fishing.

Nowadays his grandfather didn't go fishing any more, the
work of lobster creels was too heavy for him, but the old man
liked to feed the beasts in the byre, and occasionally cast an
eye on the hill to see that the twenty-one sheep were still
there. The boy and the dog went with him everywhere – you
couldn't take a boy or a dog out on the *Doo,* the fishing yole ...
His father fished alone.

Finn stood between the loch and the ocean. The winter
sun westered slowly. A few flakes came drifting down through

the bright air and glittered for a second, then died among the winter grass.

But Finn could not see his father's boat on the headland. He hoped his father would be in with his catch before sunset.

Now, on the loch, a few swans drifted, darkling.

The shadows were beginning to cluster from the east, now in mid-afternoon. The wedge of blue narrowed on the loch.

One swan drifted from the flock out into what was left of the sunlight. It trampled the loch water, it spread its wings and furled them again, it dipped its long fluent head into the water.

Ah, it was like a marvellous big pulsing star for half a minute – before shadows encroached on it too, and quenched its splendours.

And still there was no boat on the sea.

Finn was cold. He turned for home.

V

Finn's father was intent on his lobster creels, pulling them in one after the other, then he saw that the great forge-blaze of sunset was on the sea.

He did not want to be out on the night sea.

Already the knives of cold were in his blood. His hands were like blocks of ice.

But he had had a good day's work. Five boxes of lobsters! It was the richest haul of the year.

Best turn for home now, before night: before, what was worse, a snowstorm.

There, in the north-west, was the great blue-black cloud with its cargoes of snow. There were other blue-black ice-bearers under the horizon. The wind was beginning to sing, but with an undertone of threatening, a whine and a snarl.

The forge of sunset began to sink and dim.

Finn's father turned the *Doo* round, he pointed the bow for the home noust.

There – at the edge of the snow cloud, that had grown as big as a continent now – pure and lonely and bright throbbed the evening star.

The fisherman had seen Hesper ten thousand times. Tonight he actually spoke to it, 'You're bonny, right enough.'

Then the first curtains of snow were all about him.

VI

There was a bit of rowdiness in the inn bar that night.

Nobody can say for sure why one particular night in the inn should be rowdy and unpleasant, among the other three hundred storied and laughter-filled nights of the year.

But so it was, this Yule eve, of all the nights in the year.

It may have been the old rivalry between ploughmen and fishermen coming out again. It may have been that two or three of the young islanders fancied the same lass, and her name had been dropped into their contented round of stories. It could not have been because Troll the inn-keeper was more generous with his free round of whisky this Yule than usual: but no, each patron got one small dram on the house, then they were free to drink the inn dry, but at their own expense; so long as they could set silver on his counter.

Nobody knows how a fight starts exactly, from Troy to Inkerman.

It may have been Sando the beachcomber cadging drink once too often.

It may have been that the snow gale outside had gotten into their blood.

It may have been the fisherman of the *Doo* boasting about his very big catch to the other lobsterless fishermen.

Whatever the reason, a storm of abuse and flung fists and splintering glass suddenly blew up in the village inn.

Troll, a huge fat powerful man, moved in to restore order; but already the brawlers, ashamed of themselves, were disentangling themselves from the melee, and they were beginning to drift back like surly dogs to the tables they had left.

Half-a-dozen still writhed about on the flagstones of the floor.

'Think shame of yourselves,' cried Troll in his thunderous bass, 'this night of all nights!'

A pewter mug flew from somebody's fist — nobody to this day knows whose — and smashed the long mirror behind the bar, a handsome oak framed mirror that bore the legend of a famous Edinburgh brewer on it, finely scripted and scrolled.

In the centre of the mirror was a black jagged star.

VII

Finn's mother read him a story every night before bedtime.

Twenty winters ago, all the stories were spoken, but since the school had been built, it was considered the proper thing to read them out of a book.

Finn's mother was just about to light the lamp when she realised there was no oil in the bowl.

'That's vexing!' she cried. 'It's too late to go to the village shop for oil. Besides, I wouldn't trust myself in that blizzard. What a night it is! The wind's howling like wolves, out there.'

Through the bedroom window Firm could see a glimmering shadow struggling towards the byre. It was his grandfather going with the lantern to feed Tommy the ox. An extra turnip, an extra forkload of hay, to celebrate Yule.

'Where's your father?' the woman wondered, anxiously. 'He should have been home ages ago. There was a lot of noise from the inn a while back …'

Her mouth set in a bitter line whenever she spoke of the sea or the barley-freighted inn.

'I'll have to light a candle,' she said. 'I don't know what way I can read to you with a poor light like that.'

The boy was patient, longing for the enchantment of narrative. Every kind of story she read pleased him – Red Indians, pirates, Snow-White, crusaders, the sea folk … His mother had a beautiful gentle lilting voice.

In the end she took the family Bible from the deep window recess. It had big type, she could read it by the frail petal of flame.

She read the story of the three Kings crossing the desert, their camels laden with gifts for the crib in Bethlehem, following a star.

Gold, frankincense, myrrh: Firm's eyes opened wide with wonderment at the music of the words.

There was a noise downstairs: men's voices.

His mother closed the great black Bible.

She went downstairs, anxiously questioning. His father's voice answered. 'I'm home, Annie. What a night! I took Sando with me for a bowl of soup, he's cold and he's hungry. And poor Mansie, some ruffian hit him in the pub and split his lip – look, the blood on his gansy. Annie, I know you'll clean him up, he can't go home to his mother in this shape …'

The boy crept downstairs and looked – himself hidden – at the shadows in the firelight: his kind mother, and the three men reeking of salt and blood and whisky. They stood in pools of melted snow.

His mother hung the broth-pot over the fire.

'Think shame of yourself,' she said to young Mansie the fisherman, 'fighting on Christmas eve ...' But she kneaded his cold bruised fist with her warm hands.

His grandfather came in from feeding the ox, shaking snow from his coat, shouting a welcome!

Finn withdrew into the shadows.

How foolish they were, the everyday folk he knew, compared to the enchanting ones, the immortals of the stories!

He crept upstairs to his room.

The candle flame had grown tall and pure and bright. It was no wilting petal now – it seemed like the star that even now was lighting those three Kings to the snowbound city of Bethlehem.

A Candle for
Milk and Grass

The *Saturnalia* was safe. After weeks of violent eastern storms, she was safe in the harbour of Hong Kong.

My father was Lloyd's agent in the island. No sooner was the telegram in his hand than he told me to go to a certain croft on the other shore of the island. I was to tell Hubert and Annie, of Troweart, that their grandson was safe.

I reached Troweart in the last light of a winter afternoon. I knocked. Two voices bade me enter.

Old Hubert was over by the window, reading and smoking his clay pipe. There was a scattering of books and magazines in the window seat. Annie was busy between the table and the open hearth. She was baking little yellow flat cakes on a griddle. She was white with meal to the elbows.

'Magnus is safe,' I said, when I got my breath back. 'Word's just come. The ship reached Hong Kong yesterday.'

'Well, well,' she said mildly, as if I had remarked that the fire was burning bonny in the twilight. 'Well, well.'

The old man continued to read and smoke.

The little yellow cakes, fretted round the edge, gave out a sweet fragrant smell. This was the only day of the year that such cakes were made.

I sat down on a stool near the door.

★   ★   ★

'We were born too soon,' said Hubert. 'We've seen steam, and the electric telegraph, and balloons. But that's nothing to the wonders that are coming. Nothing.'

'Is that so?' I said politely. 'I'll have to be going. My mother's expecting me. It'll be tea time soon. I just came to say Magnus is well.'

'Wait a bit,' said the old man. 'Listen to this, boy. You might see it. But I won't. Nor will she.'

He bent his face upon the book. His spectacles flashed once in the firelight. He began to read in a slow grave voice.

The time is coming, is indeed not far off, when machines and energies as yet unknown and untapped will do all the work of men. Lamps will be lit without oil, a soft rich effulgence at the touch of a finger. Nor will men have to go out with ploughs and harrows and scythes, among dust and dung, in order to be nourished; nor will they be required to take the knife brutishly to beast and bird and fish. Our children will be nourished with balanced harmonious chemicals, each according to the chemical needs of his body, and none shall starve or be in want. . . .

The little sun-cakes were ready over the peat-fire. Old Annie set them, one after the other, on the clean hearth. She intoned: 'One for the table, one for the cupboard, one for a traveller, one for birds, one for the poor cold bairn.' She stood looking down at the yellow cakes with her hands clasped.

'You came between me and my book,' said Hubert. 'Do you want to be ignorant to your dying day? You have no regard for education. Keep quiet when I'm reading.'

I saw a gleam of bottles in the gathering darkness. In the far corner a little wooden bucket was seething quietly. Annie took first the ale bucket and then the chiming bottles over beside the fire. Carefully she began to decant the ale, with a jug, from bucket into bottles.

How the old man could see to read in all that cluster of shadows I do not know. His eyes were used to horizons and sheep-counts on a far hill. He resumed:

The time is coming, children will be made in the laboratories of science; they will be rational balanced healthy creatures. There is no reason why the three score years and ten of our mortality should not be multiplied four-fold, or five-fold; yea, even more....

The last dark bottle was filled and corked. Old Annie set them, one by one, against the wall. They twinkled merrily in the leaping firelight. She whispered: 'One for the fireside, one for the cupboard, one for a sad man, one for a songless man, one for the poor cold bairn.'

It was the second interruption. The old man closed his book with a clap and got to his feet. 'Annie,' he said, offended, 'I was trying to read something of importance to this boy, our visitor. I was trying to give him a vision of the day after his day. And all you do is utter that old superstitious nonsense! I'm going out....'

He did go out, into the first stars and the night-song of the sea in the west.

★   ★   ★

I got to my feet soon after that. 'Mistress Hay,' I said, 'I have to be going home, now. I just came to say, Magnus is safe.'

'A good Yule to you, boy,' said Annie.

I had to stand outside and let the darkness wash my eyes

73

for a time before I could find my way past the dwelling house. Next to it stood the byre. The byre door was open. A soft light wavered against the low flag-stone ceiling and the sharn-spattered walls. Inside, old Hubert was standing beside his one cow. In his hand he held an ox skull with a candle burning in it. The cow looked at him in wonderment.

'A good Yule to you,' said Hubert to the beast. 'Death and bread and breath. Give us butter and milk for a summer or two yet, will you?'

Christmas Visitors

The last of my Yule visitors left at ten o'clock. Thorfinn put a big peat on the fire. 'Now that'll keep you warm till you go to bed! It'll still be burning in the morning when you get up – there'll be a red glow.'

Then Thorfinn my eldest son kissed me on the forehead, and went back to his wife, who has never entered my door for ten years past.

But Thorfinn and Margaret's two children had come in the morning, or course, first thing, with their toys and presents. Pathetic little creatures! – Their faces were flushed with excitement, their mouths brimmed over with chatter. They gave me a calendar they had made themselves, with the head of a collie on it cut out of a magazine. I gave them a pound each and a glass of ginger wine. Ah, if they but knew what was in store for them: the wasted years, the husks and ashes, the salt.

And yet what more beautiful creatures, my grandchildren come in from the snow, laughing before the fire?

Harry and Sylvia put their warm red mouths against my cheek, and were eager to be out again in the snow.

And I was glad to see them go.

For I thought another visitor might come, as every year.

Loneliness is what I rejoice in now, that only: the one red-grey ember in the heart, that only a sea wind can stir into flame.

Ah, thistles, the sharp stones, salt pools, those grandchildren would have to suffer!

(She nods in her rocking chair.)

A new flame curled a yellow tongue round the peat on the hearth.

★   ★   ★

Christmas brings a few to this house still, like birds round a broken bannock.

That woman from next door came about noon, with her English voice and her English palaver and gush. I forget her name even. She came to the island two years ago for a holiday, and 'Oh, simply fell in love with the place and the people at once! . . .' So, she bought the half-ruin of the croft of Combers and has spent thousands doing it up, 'in the old traditional manner, of course − what else' − but that doesn't exclude a television and refrigerator, washing machine and central heating, and a telephone.

Separated from her husband in Birmingham − three grown-up children in different places on the globe − I have heard it all . . . She has knitted me a pair of gloves for Christmas, the tiresome woman.

And yet she has experienced miseries of which I know nothing.

There is a good-heartedness in her, buried somewhere under the gush and the flummery.

I greeted her, 'A Merry Christmas,' and I gave her a scallop shell taken from the sea bottom fifty years ago by a man called Samuel. She will crush out her cigarette ends in it.

76

★   ★   ★

They know well enough, in the farms and houses round about, that I want none of their geese and plum pudding and sherry: no invitations. A plate of my own oat bannocks and cheese, and a cup of milk – that's my Christmas dinner, and has been for years.

I was just brushing the last oat crumb from my mouth when Dawn, the ginger cat from the next farm, Colbister, came.

He shook a crumb of snow from a forefoot, delicately, in the door.

'If it isn't Dawn! What's Dawn wanting at a poor house like this, when there's goose-skin and cream in plenty up at Colbister? Well, Dawn, in the old days you'd have had a sillock or two. But there's been no fish m this house since Samuel's time. What, you could be doing with a piece of cheese? Well, then, take it.'

And the red cat ate a piece of my cheese from my fingers with the utmost delicacy and relish; and sat for five minutes at the fire blinking and washing his hind leg; and went, with the same silent courtesy as he had brought to my door.

(She drowses. The expected one is later this year.)

★   ★   ★

I think I slept in my chair most of the afternoon.

The fire sank. It was time to put a broken peat on. It was time soon to light the lamp.

I listened for a while to children singing carols in some European cathedral, on the wireless.

Such purity, such joy! The thistles, the salt, and the sharp stones, that is what you have to pay, later, for that early fountain of innocence.

Does a spring begin to flow again, late, very late, the winter before death perhaps, out of the drifted stones of the years? – a thin pure upwelling? I think not.

★   ★   ★

I had a fifth visitor. I heard a shuffle and a throat-clearing in the porch, and in he came, the oldest man in the island, Isaac, in muffler, bonnet, mittens and rubber boots.

'Isaac, what taks thee oot on a caald night like this? Thu'd been better aside thee fire. Sit doon, Isaac, till I pour thee a dram.'

When Isaac had half finished his dram he cleared his throat and he told me that once I'd been the bonniest lass in the whole island of Quoylay. 'Samuel, he was a lucky man to get thee,' says he. 'I wad have asked thee to merry me afore Samuel, only I was too shy. I just cam owre the hill to luk at thee for ten minutes or so.'

I never heard Isaac say so many words at one time. I had never got a better Christmas present in my life.

He emptied the last few whisky drops into his open mouth. Then he shambled to the door and said, 'Goodnight, lass'; and the snow and the stars took him.

(She drowses. The expected visitor has never been so late.)

★   ★   ★

Why are you so long in coming this year, Samuel? In the early years, the first grey light was hardly in the window, when you were there, pulsing from the vividness and pain of the sea! That such coldness should give me such joy! And there you stood, sea-taken one, with the piece of torn net

78

in your hand: speechless. No words passed. We delighted in each other's company. Thorfinn and Billy and Andrew slept in their cradles, with their little gifts on the chair, to await the opening of their eyes, one after the other: sea orphans. Andrew had not been born when you went in at the door of salt.

You stayed, man, while I lit the fire and hung the kettle on the hook. You were still there when I returned from the byre with the pail of warm milk. It filled the room, the light of snow and milk and bread, slowly.

Then, perhaps, one of the children rubbed the honey out of his eyes — and then you were gone, for you would never wish to harrow a child with sea-loss on a Christmas morning.

I would say, 'It's three Yules since you were lost off Yesnaby, Samuel. It joys me to see thee again. But it would be better for thee to rest soon, man' — And found I was speaking to vacancy.

'Ten Yules since you were lost, Samuel . . .' 'Seventeen Yules . . .' 'Forty-two Yules.'

When you come today, young man out of the sea to visit this old woman with cow and cabbage patch, it will be forty-three Yules since you unmoored that boat for the last time.

I think my lover will not come tonight. I pray he will not come — and yet all my year, from seedtime to harvest, is a hunger for his coming. Of late winters, his comings have been tardier and briefer. Last Yule there was but a shifting gleam, like sun reflected from ice on the wall of the yard; he was gone before the words of welcome were out of my mouth.

'Rest in peace.' An old cavernous clay-smelling skull, I will visit nobody — unless earth and sea mell and marry at the end of time.

He has come to terms with the sea-girls, I think, at last.

He will bide in their house.

At nine o'clock Thorfinn came (as I said) with a fancy -wrapped box of chocolates and a Shetland shawl – and said stale words and put the big night-lasting peat on the fire and set the cold star of his kiss on my forehead, and went away again.

(She is left with silence in the heart of her last winter: until the earth and the sea are one.)

The Children's Feast

There were twelve shops along the street of the small town: the butcher, the baker, the shoemaker, the confectioner, the grocer, the tobacconist, the draper, the fish-shop, and Mr Rousay the general merchant. (A few others were kept by old wives who sold sweeties and odds and ends.) The general merchant's was the really big shop – an emporium – and Mr Rousay sold everything – drapery, fish and flesh, needles and anchors, sweet-stuffs and groceries, knitted goods, magazines and books, ironmongery: *everything.*

In this small town by the sea, Christmas – or Yule as most folk called it – had not for a very long time been kept as a holiday. Instead, they had a wild whirl of whisky, fiddles and dancing for three days round about New Year, a week later.

It may have been the influence of a new stratum of society in the islands, the professional class (teachers, doctors, lawyers, shipping agents, excisemen) that put Yuletide in a new favourable light. At any rate, the provost, magistrates and councillors at their monthly meeting in November decided that 25 December would be a holiday, and all places of business would be closed.

Not everybody was pleased. Some of the shopkeepers said it would be bad for business – they had little enough profit as it was. The man most outspoken against this Yule holiday was Timothy Rousay, the general merchant, an elder and councillor and justice of the peace. He was reputed to be the very richest man in the town, with upwards of a thousand pounds in the bank. He it was, of all the councillors, who had moved in council against this new-fangled idle day in midwinter. And a few kirk elders muttered that popish practices were beginning to impinge. And some townsfolk said it was the English newspapers in the public library that were filling the folks' minds with all kinds of new-fangled nonsense.

But in general it was agreed that they would observe the Yule holiday – for this one year anyway, to see how it went. (In the days of their grandfathers it had been a wonderful week-long festival.)

It must be said that this particular year had been a very bad winter in Orkney, almost the worst that anyone could remember. There was deep poverty in the crofts and along the fishing piers. An appeal had been sent to Edinburgh for relief supplies to be sent north; but so far no answer had come, no deep-cargoed ship had been sighted off Hoy.

It was said that, that winter, the tinkers were better off than the smaller crofters. Being closer in touch with the sources of existence, it seemed those vagrants could wring nourishment out of stones and roots.

As for the children – when Mr Tellford the schoolmaster told them on 24 December that next day would be a holiday from school, there was in the playground an outburst of joy. A few first flakes of snow were beginning to drift down out of the early darkness. The scholars danced and cheered as if the snowflakes were a bounty of shillings and crowns. Their boots rang on the frosty cobbles.

Later the bellman walked through the street announcing at every station along the way: 'Tomorrow will be observed as a holiday in the burgh, and all shops and offices will be closed, by order of the council . . .'

Some children followed the joyous clang of the bell and the sonorous proclamation of Peter Spence the bellman all along the street. When the bellman folded his bell at the far end of the village (the last bronze echo dying away) and went into the alehouse to soothe his throat after all that outcry, there was nothing left for the kids to do but press their cold faces against the shop windows, with treasures inside of apples, chocolate, boiled sweets, cinnamon biscuits, cheese, sausages, black liquorice sticks . . .

The snow fell thicker about them. The sky was dark and there was not a star to be seen.

In one shop window a single candle glowed and dribbled in an old wine bottle. There was nothing on display, nothing at all, not so much as a fishbone or a mouldy crust. The window was empty.

But the children saw the old general merchant, Timothy Rousay, sitting at his desk inside, going through his ledger, page after page of bad debts, with a blunt pencil; sometimes scowling, sometimes smirking; often pausing to make a mark on the glimmering page.

'This beats all,' said Moll Spence at the close-end to Jemima Stevenson. 'All the shops are closed, all the offices, the six pubs and the school and the post office and the bank too. But the old skinflint is open for business as usual.'

The winged word went from end to end of the village. It was Christmas morning, and the village though deep in snow was tranced and dazzled with light, for the morning sun came flashing from the still blue harbour water and the unsullied celestial blueness.

The housewives stood round the well with their pails, pitchers, buckets, and shook their heads. 'A miser – what greed! . . .' 'It'll do him no good, the old sinner . . .' 'There's no pockets in shrouds . . .' 'Not a soul to leave it to, all his guineas and sovereigns . . .' 'Oh yes he's tempting Providence, the greedy wretch . . .' 'He'd scratch hell for a ha'penny, that man.'

So the chorus of women stood in a circle and with one voice they passed judgement on the richest man in Hamnavoe, Timothy Rousay.

★ ★ ★

A boy ran past along the street, and the scoop of his jersey that he held out with both hands was weighted to overflowing with oranges, apples and bananas.

A girl ran past with a straw basket on her arm; and the Hamnavoe housewives knew pots of syrup and jams, and packets of sugar and tea, when they saw them.

They had not time to wonder where the parents of those bairns – fishing folk – had the money to buy such delicacies, in this the poorest winter in folks' minding, when the widow's boy Pat Fara came stumbling through the snow carrying in front of him on a big plate a pig's head, with an orange in its gob.

And after Pat Fara came Johnny Cauldhame staggering under a sack of coal, and there was a Jamaica rum flask sticking out of his jacket pocket. (It was known that Johnny Cauldhame's father was bad with bronchitis, and had not been able to cut and cart peats in the summer.)

Then, a few seconds later, a boy came as if he was wearing armour, he clanged so much. Bert Kerston, challenged by the women on his homeward trudge through the snow, opened his sack and showed them a hoard of tins and cans: salmon, corned beef, rice and pears and peaches and pine-apples, beans and beetroot – all this foreign stuff that, it was said, would last forever, locked in metal. Bert Kerston took a tin-opener from his pocket and went on, laughing, to his hungry house at the end of the pier.

The women, in a wondering silence, wound their dripping buckets up from the well in the middle of the town. (And it was not often that these chatterers and keeners and legend-bearers were ever reduced to silence: the last time had been when Queen Victoria's son Alfred, Duke of Edinburgh, had walked through the street to the Town Hall – a royal prince in their midst! That had hushed their mouths like flowers for an hour till Prince Alfred in his admiral's uniform had gone aboard his launch below the Town Hall.)

The tinkers had been in their tents since early December, in the quarry at the far end of the town, and they had no money and only miscellaneous rags to keep out the bitter weather. No one wanted to buy their tin pots and spoons this winter. While the women of Hamnavoe wound up their pails of water, one after another, in a trance of silence – and each face momentarily transfigured when the sun came flashing off the trembling water surfaces – by came the tinker twins Toby and Tess, and they were laden like far-travelled merchants with coats, scarves, stockings, gloves, shawls and bonnets; and on past the well they went with their burdens of warmth as though they were bound on an expedition to Spitzbergen.

Along came Peter Spence the bellman, glum and mutinous because all the six pubs were closed. 'A disgrace,' he said. 'I'll write to the Member of Parliament . . . And all this snow. And not a drop of whisky to be had! The frost could grip a man's heart – I've heard of such a thing.'

'And why,' said Moll Spence to him sweetly, 'why, Peter man, don't you go along to Tim Rousay's shop? He's giving away things for nothing this morning. You'd get a bottle of Old Orkney malt, for sure.'

'Haven't I tried?' said the bellman. 'I pleaded with him. I offered him three shillings for a bottle, instead of the usual half-a-crown . . . And do you know what he said, the skinflint? 'Peter,' says he, 'only the bairns are getting served today.''

And Peter passed on, to try his luck at the back door of Maggie Marwick's, who kept The White Horse at the end of the village.

After that, Christmas was always observed in Hamnavoe, though the pristine purity was increasingly dulled by such things as greetings cards, decorations, paper bells, plum puddings and mince pies.

★   ★   ★

Next Christmas Timothy Rousay, councillor, kirk elder, justice of the peace – was lying in the kirkyard, and as yet no one has thought to put up a gravestone to him.

When the lawyer and the banker went through his ledger, after the funeral, they discovered that he was not a rich man at all.

He had warmed his thin blue hands at that one fire, and the children of Hamnavoe had danced round about it; and then he had said 'Goodnight' to the world and closed his door for the last time.

Three Old Men

The old man came out of his house and it was a dark night. A few snowflakes drifted on to his head.

'Well,' he said, 'I don't know why I want to leave the fire on a cold night like this. I want to get to the village but why I don't remember.'

He guessed his way along the track going down from the hill, and once he stumbled and almost fell into the wet ditch.

'Well, thank you, staff, for keeping me on my feet,' said the old man to his stick. 'A fine thing, if they found us in the morning, you and me in a drift in the ditch, as stiff and cold as one another.'

The old man laughed, and he went slowly down the cart road from the hill to the village. He felt happy, though now the snow was in his beard, and he struck out with his staff and startled a star from a wayside stone.

At the crossroads, half-way to the village, a shadow lingered. The shadow declared itself to be a man, because there was the small flame of a match being applied to a pipe. The face shone fitfully once or twice and was part of the night again.

'What's an old man like you doing out in a night like this?' said the voice at the crossroads, and the seeker in the darkness recognised Ben, the retired skipper, from the far end of the island. They had sat in the same classroom at the village school, but then they hadn't seen each other for thirty years, the time Ben was at sea, and now only occasionally at the island regatta or the agricultural show.

'The truth is,' said the old man from the hill, 'I don't rightly remember. I know I have some errand to the village, and maybe it'll come back to me before I get to the bridge.'

'Well,' said Ben, 'we might as well walk on together. I expect it's drink you're after, to keep out the cold. We can hold each other up on the way home.'

The two old men laughed. The skipper had a smell of hot rum on his breath. Could he be wanting more grog in the inn?

'I just thought,' said Ben, 'I would like to stretch my legs under the stars. Only there's not a star to be seen. It's as black as the ace of spades.'

The two old men went arm-in-arm along the track. Sometimes one or other of them would give a bark of laughter or a cry of annoyance as his foot struck against a stone in the middle of the road.

The snow was falling thicker than ever. The old sailor passed his tobacco pouch to the old shepherd, but Sam had left his pipe at home. The match spurted, and the flame showed the hollowed cheeks of Ben as he drew in the smoke, before a falling snowflake fell on the burning match – a drifting moth – and quenched it.

It was the darkest night of winter, and such a snow cloud was drifting across the island that they couldn't see the lights of the village.

But they knew the general direction.

Once they both left the road and sallied against a barbed wire fence, and one of the travellers got a deep scrape on his hand, and a fencing post knocked the burning pipe out of the other's mouth.

Then they said one or two uncomplimentary things about the farmer who had been so inconsiderate as to put up his fence in that particular place. Ben found his pipe in the snow drift. Sam shook beads of blood from his hand.

They went on, grumbling and laughing.

'I hear trouble,' said the old shepherd.

'I hear nothing,' said the old skipper, 'but then I'm hard of hearing since that last trip I made to China.'

What came to them through the darkness was music – a fragment of a reel played on a fiddle – a scratching and a scraping that could only be made by Willie the miller.

'Well,' said Willie as the skipper and the shepherd came up to him where he stood at the buttress of the bridge over the burn, 'I thought I would be playing tonight to an owl and an otter maybe. But here come two old men. Imagine that.'

On the three old men walked together. And the snow fell thicker about them.

The miller put his trembling fiddle inside his coat.

The shepherd drew his scarf across his mouth.

There was a lighthouse miles away across the Pentland Firth, in Scotland. It pulsed regularly. The sky was clear to the south.

Sometimes one or other of them would say something, but the snow muffled the words. They struggled on, arm in arm, lifting heavy feet out of the drifted ruts.

Ben said, in the ringing voice he had once used on the quarter deck, 'I think we're in for a real blizzard. I feel it in my bones.'

It was as if his words put out the lighthouse. They could see its flashings no more. The night was thickening.

They stopped at the crown of the brae to get their breath.

'I'd have been better right enough,' said the miller, 'playing this fiddle to the cat at home.'

In the slow wavering downward flake-drift their faces were three blurs.

89

'I'll tell you something,' said Ben. 'When I was in India a long while ago, I bought a piece of ivory from a merchant in Bombay. Well, I have a lot of interesting objects from all over the world at home. But this piece of ivory I always liked best. It has a bunch of grapes carved on it. Tonight I thought to myself, 'Ben, what's the use of a houseful of treasures to an old man like you? You might be dead before the first daffodils in April.' So I put the carving in my pocket and came out like an old fool into this blizzard.'

The three men stood there in the heart of the snowstorm.

'Well now,' said Sam the shepherd, 'that's a very strange thing you've said, Ben. I'll tell you why. I had three golden sovereigns put away in a stone jar on the mantelpiece. It had been there for twenty years. It was to pay for my funeral, that money. It struck me this afternoon at sunset – 'They'll have to bury you anyway, Sam,' I said to myself. 'You're too old now to mind a pauper's grave. Why don't you take the money,' said I to myself, 'and give it to the living?' . . .'

The three old men laughed, a muffled threefold merriment on the crown of the island.

The snow fell thicker still.

Willie the miller said, 'I tell you what – I've been working on a new fiddle tune since harvest. I think it's the best music I ever made. I call it *Milling the Barley*. I thought, 'I'm going to play this reel somewhere where it'll be truly appreciated' . . . But where could that be?'

'We'd better be getting on then,' said Ben.

So they linked arms and put their heads into the slow black drift. Here and there the snow was up to their knees.

'Watch where you're going,' said Willie, as if the other two were responsible for their wayward progress.

Then they were all in a deep drift, topsy-turvy, a sprawl and a welter and struggle of old men!

* * *

They got to their feet, pulling at each other, shaking the snow off their coats, wheezing and grumbling.

'I tell you what,' said Ben, 'we've lost the road altogether. We'd best go carefully. We might be over the crag and into the sea before we know.'

They could hear, indeed, the surge and break of waves against the cliff, but whether near or far-off was hard to say, on such a night.

'We're lost, that's what it is,' said Sam.

Just then the snow cloud was riven, and in a deep purple chasm of sky a star shone out, and before the cloud closed in again they saw the farmhouse Skeld with a lamp in the window.

'We're on a true bearing,' said Ben the skipper. 'But what that star was I don't know.'

The snow was falling thicker than ever as they came to the first houses of the village.

Now they could hear the hullabaloo from the inn bar, shouts and mauled bits of song and the clash and clank of pewter, and the innkeeper calling, 'Less noise! I want no rows or fighting tonight. The policeman's on his way.'

The three were aware of a lantern near the end of the kirk, and when it was near enough the lantern light splashed the face of Tommy Angel, the boy who sometimes kept the inn fires going and washed the glasses and swept the inn floor.

'I was sent to meet you,' said Tommy, 'and take you to the place.'

They could have found their own way to the inn, with all that clamour and noise coming from the lighted door.

'Lead on, Tommy,' said Sam the shepherd.

The boy led them round the inn to the byre behind, where the innkeeper stabled his beasts in winter.

The old men could just see, through the veils of snow, the glim of a candle inside.

The Lost Traveller

At last I got tired of the long theological debates in that community between the hot cliff-face and the bitter lake.

In my youth I had loved those quests into the mind and heart of God. Such subtleties, such inexorable logic had been deployed by the savants of the college! And many of them had been saintly men, who would have given their last crust to the beggar at the gate.

I had over the years been present at the death-beds of a few of such old men. It was a joy always to see with what serenity they yielded up their last breath.

But the longer I lived and studied in the community, the more it seemed to me that I had chosen a way of life too hard for me.

I looked with envy and longing at the open doors of the villages, where men sat at evening when their work in the olive groves was done, and their wives tended the fires and the cooking-pots inside, and their children ran home laughing from the hills.

Sunset made a great rose-flush over the desert, then the stars came out in a sudden shower.

Then I would turn back to the monastery door, many a night, with a pang at my heart.

Then to see, in this cell and that, the scholars sitting over their scrolls by candlelight, in the God-search that had gone on for centuries. . . .

I came to realise, as the years passed, that I did not have the dedication for such work. The delight 1 had known at the beginning was almost gone. I was a dry desert-man, and one morning I plucked a grey hair from my chin.

The kind elders of the community could not fail to notice how the ardour and joy had gone out of the man who one morning long ago had beaten on their door demanding to be made one in their brotherhood.

I had beat urgently on the panels of their door that morning. The old doorkeeper had heen a long time opening to me. The door was still trembling from my fists when he opened the door at last. 'No need for noise like that!' he said mildly. 'There's no hurry, no hurry in the world. The gates of heaven are not taken by storm. Gently, gently. Come this way. Speak in whispers. . . .' After a year of preparation they admitted me to the community. And I set out impatiently on the interior quest for God.

Now here I was, a man in middle years, lost and bewildered.

I still believed that the great Kingdom was there, and that every man and woman born must seek it in one way or another. For that pilgrimage we are born, rich and poor, high and low, the merchant and the beggar. So I tried to convince myself, over and over.

But those who come to this community are the heroic ones who seek the way by prayer, poverty, and obedience.

★ ★ ★

94

I knew at last that that was not the way for me.

The elders knew it too.

They were gentle with me. They gave me tasks to do, such as mixing mortar for the new dormitory, or seeing that the inkwells were filled and the styluses were kept sharp in the scriptorium. 'You are a good ploughman,' said an old brother to me.

'Growing corn for bread is a good way of serving God.' . . . 'Tend the vines,' he said again.

'But how I can't pray any more,' I said. 'The words in my mouth are dust.'

'Be patient,' he said. 'All shall be well.'

But the truth is, that springtime, among the lilies of the field, my spirit darkened and went out.

One morning I left the monastery. I went out of the gate under the last star as I had come, carrying nothing.

The old doorkeeper said, 'God go with you, brother.'

★ ★ ★

My father had been a wealthy wool merchant in the city, and so in my youth I had learned something of that trade.

I had no desire to go back to my father and ask to be taken on in the business. It was likely that my father was dead. And my elder brother, what would he say to a penniless tramp who turned up at his office door asking to be made a partner in the business?

I laughed, thinking of it.

In the village inn they would serve me no bread and wine, for I had no money.

A few shepherds were sitting at a table, drinking and throwing dice.

'Landlord,' said the oldest shepherd, 'give that poor man a drink. I'll settle with you.'

So I sat with the shepherds and ate and drank beside the fire.

Ah, that beer and bread was the most delicious supper I had ever tasted!

We talked together till late, the shepherds and I. I told them about my life with the brothers, and how I lost my way on the God-pilgrimage. 'And now,' I said, 'it seems to me that it is a fruitless journey in any case — there is nothing at the end of it, only death.'

'We don't worry our heads about things like that,' said one of the shepherds. 'Enjoy your beer, that's the only thing we know for sure. Landlord, bring the ale jug over here, fill the beggar-man's cup.'

We were very merry at midnight.

The shepherds asked me what I would do now, and where would I go?

I shook my head.

The oldest shepherd asked if I knew anything about sheep.

I answered that, in my boyhood, most of the talk had been about fleeces and bales and spinning, and the wool caravans that left my father's warehouse four times a year, going south towards Egypt or east to Persia.

Before the inn-keeper blew out the lamps, the shepherds had taken me on.

'We're poor men,' said Mark, the old shepherd, 'so we can't pay you much — maybe a silver piece at lambing-time and shearing-time. You'd always be sure of porridge and beer. Sat up many a night, did you, praying by candlelight? None of us likes the night-watch much. So you can sit by the fire on the hill and keep the wolf away.'

★ ★ ★

It was pleasant, sitting at the watch-fire on summer nights.

The desert below would flush red at sunset, and the stars came out like a bee swarm. Soon after that, the lights would come on in the village, and about midnight I would hear choruses from the inn.

In the north, under the horizon, sat King Herod in his palace, and in the light of his golden lamps the emerald and opal and lapis lazuli glittered.

From the small Roman outpost came, from time to time, the sound of bronze.

Away eastwards, between the crag and the bitter lake water, the small candle-flames burned in the scriptorium and in the oratory. These little lights, they often said, were man's response to the everlasting glory of God.

Not for me. The flame in my spirit was out.

From now to the day of my death I would be a shepherd who ate and laboured and slept. Such is the life that most men lead. I was content.

* * *

I had little to do at lambing-time or at the summer shearing or the arduous search for a lost sheep in the hills.

'Keep the night-watch,' they said.

They were coarse merry rough-tongued men, the shepherds. (Some I liked more than others.) They lived for their beer and dice-throwing in the village inn. Sometimes they had no money and had to bide in the tent. Some market days they got a good price for their ewes and then they drank wine in the tavern, and a few of them would get back days later, bleary-eyed.

Sometimes there would be a fist fight, and angry shouts, on the hillside. Always the old shepherd, Mark, restored order.

There was a boy they had lately taken on, a grandson of old Mark. This boy, Joachim, was left behind when the shepherds trooped down after sunset to the inn.

I was glad of Joachim's company under the stars.

As winter drew on, it was not so pleasant sitting out on that hill at night. I was thankful for the thick sheepskin over my shoulders.

More than once I saw the green eyes of the wolf at the edge of the flames. The wolf was there, then gone again.

Joachim would shout and throw stones. He would laugh as we heard the uneasy bleating of the flock and the wolf loping away in the darkness.

When the shepherds came back from the village, singing or quarrelling, Joachim boasted of how he had put the wolf to flight. 'It had a young sheep in its jaw,' said Joachim. 'I beat it on the muzzle with a stick. It dropped the sheep then. I sent the wolf away howling.'

At last the shepherds allowed Joachim to come with them to the inn. 'It's too cold now in winter up here for the boy,' said the old shepherd. 'He'd be better by the inn fire. He's too young for beer. He can have bread and cheese with us.'

I was alone then in the deepening winter.

Some nights it was so cold even the flock was silent. I could hear the growl of the wolf more than once. I could see the flash of its eyes here and there on the edge of darkness.

It was on those cold lonely vigils that I thought more and more of the brothers in their cells.

To them the earth and all the firmament proclaimed the glory of God. The humblest things were drenched through and through with the divine essence. In their silence, all created things proclaimed the eternal joy and praise.

They believed it, in their holy innocence.

I had once believed it too.

Every created thing is a messenger of God, a choiring angel.

Glory to God, sang the evening star . . . *Glory,* cried the thorn-bush . . . *Glory,* sang the stone on the road . . . *Glory,* sang the fish in the sea . . . *Glory,* sang the fire in the hearth . . . *Glory,* sang the worm under the earth . . . *Glory,* sang the waterdrops deep down in the well . . . *Glory Glory Glory* sang the mountains and the seas and the forests.

But men, who are given tongues to proclaim that glory, waste the gift of language on trivial things – on cruel laughter, on the telling of lies, on complaints and grumblings and abuse, on every kind of filth and slander, on dark covert whisperings, on cries of rage in the inn-yard after closing time.

I was sifting such thoughts through my mind when I heard Joachim calling my name. He was back early from the village.

'Come into the circle of fire, Joachim" I said, 'before the wolf gets you.'

Oh, he had so much to tell me he could hardly wait to get the words out. There was some kind of tribal assembly in the village – yokels were still coming in from all over the province – the little streets were full of noise and music, every room in the inn was taken, the landlord had had to hoist up two barrels of new wine from the cellar. It was exciting, very. . . . But the Roman soldiers billeted in the village, they did not like it, going here and there, they were on the lookout for trouble. Their hands were not far from their sword-hilts. . . . And three foreigners had spoken to Joachim, laden camels they were leading, they were wanting to know where they could stable their beasts. One of them, a black man, had given Joachim a silver coin.

'What brings you from all that carnival then?' I said.

'Well,' said Joachim, 'it's the old story. Our men, they've run out of money. And that inn-keeper, he'll give them no tick. 'No silver, no beer,' said the old gristle-snout. 'I tell you what,' he said. 'I'll give you a skin of wine for a full-grown lamb – how about that?' You know the lamb that was born in the first snow. Well, the shepherds told me to fetch down that lamb. So here I am.'

Glory to God, cried the lamb slung across Joachim's shoulders. And *Glory* sang the star over the desert. And *Glory* proclaimed the fire beside the sheepfold. (My ear of clay did not hear it – but on such a night it seemed such universal joy might be possible.)

'The shepherds told me,' said Joachim, 'to take you down to the feast. "The fire can look after itself for one night", they said. "That holy man can do with some cheering up", they said. So hurry.'

'It's a marvellous night' said Joachim as I was thonging the cord at the neck of my sheep-skin coat. 'Glory be to God' he sang.

★ ★ ★

So it was that the God-seeker who had lost his way went down at midnight to the inn.

One Christmas in Birsay

A Story

Two boys were down in the ebb at Birsay, they moved from rockpool to rockpool, probing. Their faces looked back at them from the still mirrors, with the winter-blue sky behind. Then one of the boys put his foot in a tassle of seaweed and he slithered and half fell into a rockpool with a small splach.

'Watch where you're going, Magnus,' said the other boy. 'The man who looks always at the sky will have a fall....'

The sleeve and breeches of the boy, when he got out of the pool, were soaking. But he laughed, shaking a shower of salt from his clothes.

'In an hour,' he said, 'there'll be no rockpools to fall into. The sea's coming in fast.'

The sea-wet boy found a scallop shell.

The other boy found a broken oar-blade. 'This must be the longship that was lost in the storm last week.'

'A scallop shell is a sign of pilgrimage,' said the boy called Magnus. 'Listen to the surge out there, the sea-songs. If we don't go up to the Hall soon, we'll have to swim ashore.'

'The old grandfather will be sitting over the fire,' said the boy with the broken oar. 'Will he be able to go to the church tonight? Will Thorfinn know that it's Christmas-eve?'

*   *   *

The two boys did not sit long over the mid-day meal. It was fish and thin beer. The old earl, their grandfather, did not come to the table. A woman knelt beside him with a bowl and put pieces of fish into his mouth. 'That's enough,' said Earl Thorfinn. 'I'm not hungry. I'm cold, though. Put more logs on the fire'....

The two boys went over to greet their grandfather.

'Who are you?' said Thorfinn Sigurdson. 'Where have you come from? I don't know you.'

'I'm Hakon,' said the elder boy.

'I'm Magnus,' said the other.

'Don't stand between me and the fire,' said the old man. 'Boys ought to be out in the wind and sun. You'll draw to the hearth soon enough.'

The boys turned and ran out of the hall. They passed a man with a scroll, who bowed to them. The scribe was going to read some lines of saga to the Earl. 'I ought to be reading scripture to him,' said the scribe to the boys. 'He'll have nothing but voyages and sieges. I don't think he knows it's Christmas. He'll fall asleep, for sure, in the middle of the reading'....

*   *   *

The mid-winter sun would be down in an hour.

Soon the two boys would have to go back indoors.

They could see how busy the clergy were in the church. Tonight there would be more than one service in the church. Evensong and Compline before the Mass of the Nativity at

102

midnight. The bishop stood in the door of the church. He raised his hand to the boys.

The two boys climbed to the summit of the steep green island. It was a still winter afternoon. The globe of the sun hung low on the horizon. The sea ran gold, then crimson as blood.

They stood together, their arms on each other's shoulders, looking out over the ocean. Already, from the north, darkling shadows moved on the flood.

They were attacked by a bird! Suddenly out of the sunset it came at them, there on the clifftop – a threshing and flurry and beat of wings, a frenzy of beak and claws.

The two boys were so startled they fell back, arms before faces, separately.

The bird went after the boy Hakon. He turned and ran, helter-skelter. Then, remembering that the pulse of sea-kings beat in him, he picked up a large stone and hurled it at the bird. The stone missed, but the bird rode higher on the wind and turned and fell on the boy Magnus who stood where he was, on the cliff-edge. The bird fell about the boy's head with shrieks and a concentrated fury of wings. And still the boy stood.

Hakon covered his eyes.

From the church below – in a time and place far removed – he heard the plainsong.... *The torrent would have swept over us: over us then would have swept the raging waters.*

Blessed be the Lord, who did not leave us a prey to their teeth....

Hakon dug another stone out of the turf and turned to help his friend.

What he saw, black against the glow in the south-west, was the bird sitting furled on the outstretched hand of Magnus.

When Hakon approached, the bird opened its wings and flew unhurriedly out over the waves.

Then Hakon saw that there was a fresh claw-mark on his friend's forehead, and blood was seeping and dropping from

103

the wound.

'Time to get back,' said Magnus. 'Look, a lantern in the byre door.'

★   ★   ★

A chair had been brought into the church, for the old Earl to sit on. But nobody thought he would come.

A Birsay farm boy lit the candles on the altar.

Another farm boy climbed into the belfry. He rang the bell to summon the people to the Mass of the Nativity. They came slowly, in little groups, crofters and fishermen and wives and children; they stood here and there in the little cold church.

Something wonderful would happen soon.

The palace officials entered – falconer and the keeper of the horses and the three skippers and the treasurer and the scrivener and the king's man from Norway and the beautiful lady Thora. They came in one by one and genuflected and stood near the altar.

Two boys came in – those who would be earls some day – and the common people saw that one of the boys had a bandage round his head. The boys knelt one on each side of Thora.

There was a stir at the door. The old Earl Thorfinn Sigurdson was entering. Two men hovered about him, in case he should stumble, One took him lightly by the elbow and pointed to the carved chair over by the altar.

The old man paid no attention. Painfully he knelt down at the back of the church, among the croft-folk and the fisher-folk.

Plainchant drifted from the young mouths in the choir. *Dominus dixit ad me: Filius meus es tu, ego hodie genui te.*

The young bishop entered, William, with three boys to serve at the Mass of the Nativity.

Birds called from the enfolding waters below.

The church seemed to be afloat suddenly on a tide of joy.

.

The Feast of the Strangers

An Orkney fable

When the days got very dark, in the middle of winter, the woman who lived in the croft down at the shore, was never happy till her three sons were home and the door was shut for the night. Then the lamp was lit and the peat-fire blown into flame. They ate their supper and were in bed long before midnight.

The woman had reason to fear winter. The previous January her husband and two neighbours had gone fishing. A sudden storm came out of the north. The boat had never returned.

By good fortune her eldest boy Peter had newly learned to handle a boat and to fish with his father. Now Peter was the breadwinner. Yet she dreaded that the sea might take him too, some day.

The second boy, Sam, was the joy of her heart He knew everybody in the island; he was welcome at nearly every door. Even the laird's sour-faced sister would take Sam in from his wanderings about the roads and give him ginger-bread and lemon water. He would come back to the croft after a long day and tell his mother and brothers all the news he had heard. He told the stories so drolly, and with such fine mimicry of the island voices, that they had to laugh. Even Gib laughed. Sam, the mother knew, would be a good ploughman, a good provider, in a year or two.

Gib was the youngest boy. The less said about him the better. The island folk said of Gib that he was 'trowie'— that is, the trows (or trolls) must have stolen the true child and left Gib — one of their own offspring — in the cradle instead. All he was allowed to do was feed the beasts. Some nights he slept in the byre himself.

'NOW,' said the minister in the kirk one Sunday, 'it's getting on for Yule, the very darkest time of the year. But this is the time that the Lord of All chose to give us men a very precious gift, his own Son' . . . Then he read to them out of his big black Bible the story of the Nativity, which of course they knew by heart already. 'We must be thinking,' said he, 'of some way of showing our gratitude for that gift. We should put ourselves in the place of those three kings who came to the village where the Child was, bringing gifts. Let us seriously think of the gifts we can bring to the church next Friday and the days following . . .'

★   ★   ★

The days dwindled and darkened down to the solstice, but remained calm, so that Peter was able to go fishing every day. On the Thursday Gib said to Peter: 'Peter, I want to come out in the boat with you, to catch a few fish.'

'You will not,' said his mother sharply. 'A boat is dangerous enough without a clumsy creature like you in it.'

Gib said: 'All right then, mother.'

Gib wandered away to a neighbouring farm, where a bad-tempered man called Jacob Taing lived.

'Mr Taing,' said Gib. 'do you remember when I helped in your oatfield at harvest? You forgot to pay me a wage.'

'You – a wage!' said Jacob Taing. 'You were a hindrance to everybody! You got in the way of the scythes. Away home with you.'

But Mrs Taing took Gib into the house. She brought a barley scone out of the cupboard, broke it in five pieces, and wrapped them up.

'There's your harvest wages, Gib,' she said. 'A good Yule to you, when it comes.'

Gib went home with his bread.

★　★　★

When Peter returned before sunset, Gib was standing on the shore. Peter set down a box of fish on the rock. He gave two haddocks to Gib. 'That's for you, Gib,' he said. 'That's for keeping the sea calm for me. There's a storm breeding in the north – look!' There was a blue-black bruise indeed on the northern horizon.

Gib walked up to the house with his two haddocks.

★　★　★

Sam came back red-cheeked, from the heart of the island, just after sunset when there was still a lingering redness in the west. He could hardly wait to tell them the news. 'There's wandering folk in the island,' he said. 'Strangers. I didn't see them myself. They're among the hills. They're living in an old patched tent. The factor's on the lookout with his dog and gun – he's going to clear them out. They have no business in the island at all. . . .'

After supper, while they were sitting round the fire, the mother said: 'Tomorrow's Yule. I have a shilling put by, a gift to the Lord. You, Peter, will have to give something too.'

Peter said he had a sixpenny piece put by, ever since the big haul of lobsters in summer.

Sam, tired out, was sleeping in the chair.

Gib asked his mother if she remembered how he had helped her on the peat-hill the summer before. The mother said: 'You got in everybody's way! You fell in a peat bank and you were as black as Satan, and half-drowned, when I dragged you out!'

'I want three peats for my day's wages,' said Gib.

Sam woke up and immediately remembered about the dark strangers. 'Everybody's frightened,' he said. 'Every croft's going to bar its door tonight.'

'I will too,' said the mother. 'I'll bar my door.'

'The good weather's at an end,' said Peter. I won't get to the fishing this side of Hogmanay. God help any poor folk with no roof over their heads!'

Even as he spoke, the first gust struck the end of the croft house. The door shook. The smoke wavered in the hearth.

Gib said he would sleep in the byre that night. His mother said he would be safer in the house. There were those strangers in the island. The byre door had no bar to it.

But Gib lifted his two fish from the blue stone floor. He found his parcel of bread in the cupboard. He lifted three peats from the basket beside the hearth. Then he went out into the black loud night.

'That boy!' said the mother. 'What does he want with peats and bread and haddocks in a byre! He hasn't even waited for the good words to be said.'

Peter held up his hand. He chanted 'the good words' – 'May we thy servants and all the creatures in this croft hide in the care and keeping of thy angels till morning.'

Pete and Sam went to bed then. The woman of the house

dimmed the flame of the lamp. She glanced through the window at the dark howling night. She barred the door. Then she looked towards her bed.

★ ★ ★

There was a lamentation of storm over the island all that night. Old folk couldn't sleep for the noises of wind and sea.

In the first light of morning, when Peter looked through the pane the Sound was all gray and black and white.

Sam could hardly wait to get into his coat. He knew how he would pass the morning – Yule greeting after Yule greeting! – the wind and the boy's shout in every door! In most of the houses Sam would be given a little 'sun-cake' and a spoon of honey, beside the Yule fire.

His mother unbarred the door for him, and kissed him, and let him go.

★ ★ ★

Gib didn't come in for his breakfast. The mother thought nothing of that. He would speak to the ox for an hour on end, some days. She was busy all morning preparing a good Yule dinner – ham broth, a stuffed and roasted duck, and 'sun-cakes.'

Sam returned from the farms at noon burdened with presents he had got – pennies, little wooden toy beads, pigs' bladders for playing football. And he was hungry ...

The mother called from the open door 'Dinner!' Soon Peter came up from the shore, where he had been making the boat secure.

But Gib, where was he – the 'trowie one' – where was the bitter cross she had to bear (though she loved him too in her way)? Surely he didn't mean to spend the whole day in the byre!

110

'Dinner!' she called again. Still there was no sign of Gib.

She went angrily to the byre door.

Inside there was such brightness, such a piercing fragrance, such minglings of pure grave sweet sound, that she cried out and covered her face.

When she took her hands from her face at last, it was the byre as she had always known it. The cow and the ox munched hay. Gib leaned against the door-post, happy to share the four walls with those friends of his.

Where the light and the incense and the music had been there was nothing – except, on the stone floor, some hot peat ashes, and a crumb or two, and fish bones.

The Lost Boy

There was one light in the village on Christmas Eve; it came from Jock Scabra's cottage, and he was the awkwardest old man that had ever lived in our village or in the island, or in the whole of Orkney.

I was feeling very wretched and very ill-natured myself that evening. My Aunty Belle had just been explaining to me after tea that Santa Claus, if he did exist, was a spirit that moved people's hearts to generosity and goodwill; no more or less.

Gone was my fat apple-cheeked red-coated friend of the past ten winters. Scattered were the reindeer, broken the sledge that had beaten such a marvellous path through the constellations and the Merry Dancers, while all the children of Orkney slept. Those merry perilous descents down the lum, Yule eve by Yule eve, with the sack of toys and books, games and chocolate boxes, had never really taken place at all I looked over towards our hearth, after my aunt had finished speaking: the magic had left it, it was only a place of peat flames and peat smoke.

I can't tell you how angry I was, the more I thought about it. How deceitful, how cruel, grown-ups were! They had exiled my dear old friend, Santa Claus, to eternal oblivion. The gifts

I would find in my stocking next morning would have issued from Aunty Belle's 'spirit of generosity.' It was not the same thing at all. (Most of the year I saw little enough of that spirit of generosity – at Halloween, for example, she had boxed my ears till I saw stars that had never been in the sky, for stealing a few apples and nuts out of the cupboard, before 'dooking' time.)

If there was a more ill-tempered person than my Aunty Belle in the village, it was, as I said, old Jock Scabra, the fisherman with a silver ring in his ear and a fierce one-eyed tom cat.

His house, alone in the village, was lit that night. I saw it, from our front door, at eleven o'clock.

Aunty Belle's piece of common sense had so angered me, that I was in a state of rebellion and recklessness. No, I would *not* sleep. I would not even stay in a house from which Santa had been banished. I felt utterly betrayed and bereaved.

When, about half past ten, I heard rending snores coming from Aunty Belle's bedroom, I got out of bed stealthily and put my cold clothes on, and unlatched the front door and went outside. The whole house had betrayed me – well, I intended to be out of the treacherous house wflien the magic hour of midnight struck.

The road through the village was deep in snow, dark except where under old Scabra's window the lamplight had stained it an orange colour. The snow shadows were blue under his walls. The stars were like sharp nails. Even though I had wrapped my scarf twice round my neck, I shivered in the bitter night.

Where could I go? The light in the old villain's window was entrancing – I fluttered towards it like a moth. How would such a sour old creature be celebrating Christmas Eve? Thinking black thoughts, beside his embers, stroking his wicked one-eyed cat.

The snow crashed like thin fragile glass under my feet.

113

I stood at last outside the fisherman's window. I looked in.

What I saw was astonishing beyond ghosts or trows.

There was no crotchety old man inside, no one-eyed cat, no ingrained filth and hung cobwebs. The paraffin lamp threw a circle of soft light, and all that was gathered inside that radiance was clean and pristine: the cups and plates on the dresser, the clock and ship-in-the-bottle and tea-caddies on the mantel-piece, the framed picture of Queen Victoria on the wall, the blue stones of the floor, the wood and straw of the fireside chair, the patchwork quilt on the bed.

A boy I had never seen before was sitting at the table. He might have been about my own age, and his head was a mass of bronze ringlets. On the table in front of him were an apple, an orange, a little sailing ship crudely cut from wood, with linen sails, probably cut from an old shirt. The boy – whoever he was – considered those objects with the utmost gravity. Once he put out his finger and touched the hull of the toy ship; as if it was so precious it had to be treated with special delicacy, lest it broke like a soap-bubble. I couldn't see the boy's face – only his bright hair, his lissom neck, and the gravity and joy that informed all his gestures. These were his meagre Christmas presents; silently he rejoiced in them.

Beyond the circle of lamp-light, were there other dwellers in the house? There may have been hidden breath in the darkened box bed in the corner.

I don't know how long I stood in the bitter night outside. My hands were trembling. I looked down at them – they were blue with cold.

Then suddenly, for a second, the boy inside the house turned his face to the window. Perhaps he had heard the tiny splinter-ings of snow under my boots, or my quickened heart-beats.

The face that looked at me was Jock Scabra's, but Jock Scabra's from far back at the pure source of his life, sixty winters

114

ago, before the ring was in his ear and before bad temper and perversity had grained black lines and furrows into his face. It was as if a cloth had been taken to a tarnished web-clogged mirror.

The boy turned back, smiling, to his Christmas hoard.

I turned and went home. I lifted the latch quietly, not to awaken Aunty Belle – for, if she knew what I had been up to that midnight, there would have been little of her 'spirit of generosity' for me. I crept, trembling, into bed.

When I woke up on Christmas morning, the 'spirit of the season' had loaded my stocking and the chair beside the bed with boxes of sweets, a *Guinness Book of Records,* a digital watch, a game of space wars, a cowboy hat, and a 50 pence piece. Aunty Belle stood at my bedroom door, smiling. And, 'A merry Christmas,' she said.

Breakfast over, I couldn't wait to get back to the Scabra house. The village was taken over by children with apples, snowballs, laughter as bright as bells.

I peered in at the window. All was as it had been. The piratical old man sluiced the last of his breakfast tea down his throat from a cracked saucer. He fell to picking his black-and-yellow teeth with a kipper-bone. His house was like a midden.

The one-eyed cat yawned wickedly beside the new flames in the hearth.

A Haul of Winter Fish

To DAVE BROCK

Storm and blizzard over Hamnavoe – storm and snow day after day as the light dwindled down towards midwinter.

The storm from the north had roused the sea to great snarling crested billows. It would have been madness for the Hamnavoe fishermen to put out in such weather. Hunger could be endured. The loss of men and fishing boats was a thing not to be thought of.

So the poor families ate the dried sillocks from last summer. The three shopkeepers would give them no more credit; there was enough debt against the fishing houses in their ledgers.

No good going to the farms and crofts round about. The crofting families were as poor as themselves, almost.

The storm raged on. At night, during a blizzard, one Hamnavoe house couldn't see the light in the window of the house on the next pier, through the dark whirls.

Time was like a wick in an almost exhausted lamp, as Yule drew close.

The time darkened down towards Yule.

★ ★ ★

The boy from the very poorest house in Hamnavoe was standing, after sunset, at the edge of his father's pier. In the lull between two blizzards a patch of sky had shredded thin. A star shone through rags of cloud, bright as a nail.

Beyond Hoy, he could hear the shifting muted thunders of the Atlantic.

The star put a thin lustre on the darkening heave of harbour water. The fishing boats were drawn high on the nousts, safe as gulls in crag crannies.

An abandoned hook on the edge of the small pier took the light of the star; the barb glittered diamond-bright for a second.

Then the wind roused itself with a clap of hands and a black yell.

The first flakes of a new blizzard danced all about the boy.

The star was quenched, suddenly.

He turned. He went into his house.

The family sitting round the hearth-fire turned flushed story-rapt faces to his cold face.

His mother said. 'So that's it – you'd rather be out in the black night than sitting with your family round the fire. At Yule too! A strange boy – you've always been a strange boy.'

He said nothing.

'There's no more food, the pot's empty! In the morning we're going to the Kirk Rocks for seafood. You'd better get to bed – it's an early start. Old grand-da's tired with telling stories.'

The boy brought the coldness and darkness of winter into the fire-circle and the story-glutted faces.

Grand-da, the harp of his mouth still trembling, lighted his pipe.

The fire fingered gold through the hair of the boy's three sisters.

The little one slept in his crib in a corner; time pulsed softly

117

through him, like fish in the fathomless depths.

'There's one piece of news,' said the boy. 'I saw a boat. It came out of Hoy Sound into the harbour just at the time of the first stars. I never saw that yawl before. A black man came up the steps of our pier, he was carrying a heavy basket of fish. He shouted to two men in the boat below. They passed up to him two more baskets of fish. The black man set the three baskets on our pier. He never said a word. Then he and the two other foreign-looking men (one with a gold ring in his ear) walked on up to the ale-house. And that's the end of the story.'

'Get to your bed,' cried the mother. 'You and your dreams! Some fisherman you'll be when you grow up. To bed with you. It's an early start for us all. A seaweed dinner for Yule, if we're lucky.' . . .

★   ★   ★

When the mother opened the door in the morning, upon the jet and crimson of dawn over Scapa, there were three brimming baskets of cod on the pier: enough to feed every house in the village.

The storm was over – the harbour flashed, all azure and silver.

Her cry of amazement brought all the family to the door – three sleepy-eyed yellow-haired girls, the bitter fisherman who had caught no fish since December came in, old grand-da with his pipe in his hand.

Inside the child cried: a small star of wonderment.

From the neighbouring piers groups of fisher folk watched.

They called – bright shivering words. They held out their hands towards the baskets of fish.

Only the boy slept on in the box bed – the dreamer – as if he had been drawing in heavy lines all night in a rough sea westward.

The Christmas Horse

'If you want to write to Santa Claus, write to him,' said Mrs Sabiston. 'There's a writing pad and pencil in the drawer.'

'I will, then,' said peedie Billy, 'all I want is a horse.'

Annie, his sister, who was twelve, sniggered, putting on her coat and scarf.

'Leave the boy alone,' said Mrs Sabiston, quite severely.

Annie, still laughing, went outside among the first stars and snowflakes.

Billy, aged eight, sat under the paraffin lamp, and it took him as long to compose the Christmas letter as it might have taken the gravestone maker to cut an inscription.

His mother mixed the Christmas pudding. The little croft among the Orkney hills brimmed with spices and fruits of the Orient.

Dear Santa, wrote Billy. *Please can I get a horse for Christmas, just leave it at the end of the house as I know it won't be easy for you to put a horse in my stocking.*

I like horses more than anything. Just a horse will do, never mind fruit or sweeties.

Yours, William Sabiston junior.

His mother had made a very rich sphere of the pudding and was about to wrap it in its cloot. The biggest pot in the house was chuckling on top of the stove.

'Won't you read the letter to me?' said Mrs Sabiston, now that Billy had laid aside the blunt pencil and torn the script out of the pad.

'Oh no,' said peedie Billy. 'Letters is private.'

Meantime, Annie had come in from the first snowfall and her eyes were two glittering stars and her cheeks were two apples, and she was a galaxy of snow crystals from head to feet.

Peedie Billy put his letter to Santa into the fire and a flame licked it up in an instant.

'What way on earth,' said Annie, 'is Santa going to read a burnt letter?'

'Don't torment the boy,' said his mother. 'Time for your homework.'

'It doesn't matter anyway,' said Annie. 'Because there's no such person as Santa.'

Peedie Billy gave his sister a look of wonderment and pity.

Then he stood in the open door for a while looking at the dark hills where he would ride his horse on summer days.

Then he yawned and mumbled 'goodnight' to his mother and sister and went to bed. Sleep bore him off with slow-sifting mane and gentle hoof-beats.

The pudding sang happy songs and thumped and thumped in the black pot.

There had never been a Christmas morning like it in the croft.

Peedie Billy had rushed out at first light to welcome his horse. And the field was empty. Nor was there a sign of a horse in byre and barn, or anywhere about the steading.

He came indoors, downcast. His sister Annie was in her nightgown, turning the pages of a new book with illustrations called *Little Women*. Annie was very pleased with her Christmas present. As she turned the pages she chomped on her Christmas apple and peeled bits of Spanish sunshine from her Christmas orange.

Peedie Billy's stocking was loaded too. He pulled out an apple, an orange and a wooden horse painted bright red with black spots, and it stood on a kind of platform with a wooden wheel at each corner.

Mrs Sabiston came in from milking the cow upon a disgraceful scene. Peedie Billy had thrown the toy horse against the wall with such force that the wheels had come off and the head was bashed in. Annie sat in the rocking chair, laughing. Peedie Billy, in a passion of tears, threw first his apple and then his orange at his sister.

'What a way to carry on,' cried Mrs Sabiston, 'on Christmas morning!'

The rest of the day, however, was happy enough.

Neighbours dropped by and one of them – the blacksmith – gave peedie Billy a shilling. 'A horse!' said the blacksmith, when he had drunk his glass of Old Orkney. 'You'll never want for a horse, boy. I can tell a good horseman when I see one. You have the very hands of a ploughman, Billy.'

'You'll be a famous horseman some day. You will that.'

Three neighbour women came in and kissed him under the mistletoe, one after the other, amid a storm of laughter, and they gave him sixpence each.

Soon it was dinner time and peedie Billy enjoyed the goose and tatties, and he ate so much of the pudding that he thought for a while he would burst. The ginger wine glowed on his tongue with all the magic fires of winter.

Annie said not one word all day. She sat curled in the rocking chair reading *Little Women*. She was still reading it when her mother lit the lamp in the middle of the afternoon.

Peedie Billy wandered outside in the first dark. Maybe Santa was late with his horse. Maybe it would be waiting at the end of the steading for him, cold, wanting a mouthful of hay.

But there was still no horse under the stars.

★ ★ ★

The night before Hogmanay the boy sat writing a letter at the table.

Annie was making a rag doll for the poor blind child in the croft house beside the loch. She could be a kind enough girl to people outside the family.

The mother was mixing shortbread in an immense bowl beside the fire. The whole parish, even the W.R.I. women, said Mrs Sabiston was the best woman for shortbread they knew. There wouldn't be much of her shortbread left by the sixth of January.

Peedie Billy finished the letter and addressed it and put it in the stove and ran outside under the freezing stars.

The letter, half scorched, fell through the ribs of the stove and smouldered on the stone floor.

Annie fell on it like a gull on a crust of bread. It was addressed to Mr S. Claus

Dear Sir, (Annie read aloud), *the horse I got for Christmas was not the kind of horse I was thinking about when I wrote to you. I hope you forgive me for the way I treated the wooden horse. Andrew Stout the joiner has mended it, thank you for same. Sam the blacksmith says it takes a long while for a good horse and a good horseman to meet up with each other, so I'll just be patient. I'm sorry for calling you an old cheat and a twister on Christmas morning, but I was really mad.*

Yours faithfully, William Sabiston, junior . . .

Annie could hardly get the last words out, rolling about among the rags and scissors and spools of thread, shrieking with mirth.

I would not have you forget that I am speaking about an incident in the childhood of the most famous horseman in his day, in Orkney, Shetland and Caithness: William Sabiston of Thorstone. He won every ploughing match between the ages of 18 and 40. No man, it was said, drove a purer furrow. Wherever in the north-east there was a sick horse or an intractable horse, William Sabiston was sent for. There was a healing in his look, and in his words and in his hands.

His own horses were splendid animals. There they stood, heraldic against the sunset, or, sniffing a storm out in the Atlantic, they tossed their manes and the thunder of their hooves echoed from the laird's hall to the fisherman's bothy.

The sideboard up at Thorstone farm was crowded with silver trophies. Visitors who came to call on the elderly master of horses thought it strange to see, among the engraved silver pieces, a toy wooden horse with rickety wheels and only one eye.

It's said, the old man died on the day the first tractor was unloaded from the Aberdeen boat on to the pier at Kirkwall.

The Last Island Boy:
A Story for Christmas

'Christmas!' said the man. 'What do we want with Christmas? What's Christmas to us? All I know is, it's winter. The worst storms are still to come. Will we last through the winter? That's what I'd like to know.'

The woman said nothing. She put a few pieces of salt fish into the pot and began to peel potatoes.

Outside, it was another grey cold day. Sometimes the greyness outside would darken, as if another shadow or cloud had been mixed into it. Then sleet would blatter on the window for a while, a bleak, cold sound.

'We should never have come here in the first place,' said the man. 'It hasn't worked. But if I hadn't come – if I hadn't left that office in Leeds and come, I would be tormenting myself still with the dream – the island of innocence and peace in the North, face to face with the elements. That, I thought in my ignorance, was how people should live . . .'

The boy had just been ferried across from the bigger island that had the school on it. From the few lights on the pier he had been ferried, the sole passenger, to the lamp in the solitary island croft.

'It's just that they're having a Christmas party in the school,' he said.

The woman broke another peat into the range and stirred the ribs till a new flame appeared.

'Come over and warm yourself,' she said.

*   *   *

The next day was Saturday. The boy lay warm in the nest of his bed till nine o'clock.

When he got up and went into the kitchen the lamp was still lit. The woman was baking at the table. Her face was flushed. It seemed to be a different baking from the usual Saturday morning oatcakes and floury bannocks. There were three stone jars on the table. She was intent on a cookery book. The whole stove seemed to throb with the red glow of the peat.

'There's tea in the pot,' said the woman. 'The porridge is a bit cold.'

'Where is he?' said the boy.

'He's out in the boat,' said the woman. 'There's a storm forecast. He wants to get a few fish if he can."

It was a much better morning. The night wind had swept the sky clear of the last rag of cloud. The sky was a delicate blue, like china. The sun was low in the south-east, making silver undulations on the rise and fall of the sea.

'Goodness!' cried the woman, 'the sun's out . . .' She screwed down the wick and blew out the lamp flame with a small spurt of breath.

The boy wandered outside, among a quick welcome and dispersal of hens (because they saw he had no food for them).

He had the whole morning to himself. He wondered if it would be possible, before dinner-time, to visit every ruined croft in the island . . . No, it wouldn't be possible. The midwinter sun would be down before he had half completed his round, and he might not find his way home again.

Still, he would manage six or seven.

The first croft, Smert, wasn't far away, across two fields and a wet ditch. It was still in passable shape, Smert. An island family had lived there till two years before, then suddenly they had sold up and gone to live in the town. The croft had been advertised for sale. Nobody had wanted it. (Who would want to live and work in a dying island?)

But for his dark resolute father, there were no crofters in the island now.

The boy peered through the window of Smert. There was a table and two chairs inside, a box bed, a rusted range; a picture of the Channel Fleet on one wall. But the place breathed dampness and decay.

The boy left Smert and ran towards the next croft. It was an utter ruin. He did not know what its name was. Naked rafters showed through the few roofing flags that remained. Door and windows were vacant rectangles. Long and low the croft lay on the first slope of the hill, as if it had sailed forever on that green wave from the foundation-stone to the first sag of the roof: Ten generations maybe. Beyond the living-quarters lay the remnants of byre and barn; the floor a confusion of stones.

And yet, thought the boy, there was a freshness and cleanness about it, like a bone in the wind and rain, now that the last rags and shards of life were no longer there.

The nameless place must have been deserted for half-century at least.

From the top of the low island hill the boy could see seven or eight other islands. His own island was spread beneath him like a drab brown cloth, pitted with ruins and half-ruins, and a few mounds from the very ancient past.

The winter sun had reached its zenith and in another three hours would go, a cold bright diamond, into the Atlantic.

Ah, there was the boat, under the cliff, with the man in it! He was leaning over and looking deep into the sea, one oar upraised.

And there she was, the woman, outside the door, throwing cold porridge and bread-crumbs and oats to the hens.

(Since the time of the poor harvest, they had stopped using names. 'The man,' 'the woman,' 'the boy' — that's how they referred to each other.)

He drifted down, slowly, to the biggest house in the island, the laird's hall. The tall house was stubborn in its fight against time. The great door still stood, and the shutters, though the paint had long since peeled from them and they were beginning to warp. But the stonework — it could outface centuries, so firmly the masonry had been dressed and set. The walls of the great garden, too, showed not a breach or a fissure, though the garden itself — once plotted into a formal Italian style by two gardeners from the South — was a jungle of weeds and nettles.

The tall octagonal sundial intrigued the boy. Last summer the indicator had thrown the sun's shadow on precisely, the right mark. The wet autumn had corroded it, and time fell a blank on the stone's intricate angles.

Here, in the great drawing-room, there would have been winter balls a hundred years ago, rustling of silk gowns, music of violin and piano, old formal courtesies of invitation and acceptance, smells of Havana cigars, hot punch, trout, grouse.

Standing on tiptoe outside the tall window, the boy felt a desolation he had not known before. Where was it now, all that wealth and beauty? When had the roses and butterflies left the garden?

He ran, squelching through a wet field to the shore. Well, he had heard all about this ruin and its former tenant. It had been

127

called 'Jamaica' and Captain Haraldson had lived there between his retirement from the sea until he went on his last voyage to the hospital, and soon into the deeper waters of death.

The islanders said he hadn't been a skipper at all; an ordinary seaman all his career, at best maybe boson. And the left forearm he said had been taken by a shark – that, said the last islanders, had been the result of a wild punch-up in Amsterdam in his youth.

'That shark,' the skipper had said, 'he had my arm, but I had his life – I ripped him open from fin to tail! . . .' And the wives he had had, in the Gilbert Islands and San Francisco and St John's, and the horde of children, scattered world-wide. 'It's a funny thing,' old widow Wilson had said, 'whenever he came on leave, not a lass would look at him, in this island or that.'

The ruin of the skipper's house stood right on the edge of the sea-banks. Erosion was eating so fast into this part of the shore, that a cornerstone of the house was actually overhanging the edge of the shallow cliff. It would not be very long, thought the boy, till all those stones would be mingled with the shore stones and the sea.

He wondered where the old sailor had sat and told his stories. Over there it must be, in a chair, beside that blackened stone, the hearth. He stooped and turned a stone. The sun through the broken west wall took a dull gleam from a coin! The boy picked it up. It had strange devices on either side, and foreign lettering. Was it – could it conceivably be – gold? It was yellow and untarnished. Had the skipper hidden it away for some purpose? Had it fallen out of his coin-box one night and rolled into an interstice of the flagstone floor?

Whatever had happened, it was a marvellous thing to have found! He would carry it home. Perhaps it would save them from the ruin that the man said was staring them in the face . . .

128

The thought that next year the island might be utterly empty put a shiver of fear over him.

He stowed the coin carefully in his pocket.

Across the Sound he could see the island where he went to school five mornings a week. He looked. Yes, there it was, the big building at the back of the village, between the church and the shop. As he looked, the declining sun flashed from the school window, suddenly, intolerable brightness, as if the interior was a mass of cold silver flames.

He walked along the shore, eastwards. A few skeletons of fishing boats rotted among the stones. He could just make out the name of one boat: STAR.

Going up the shore path to the road above, he passed the green mound with its few underground dwellings where the archaeologists from England had worked all last summer. There, in stone hollows not so very different from the crofts of recent times, had lived the first islanders of all, with their fish-oil lamps and clay pots or grain and milk.

But were they really the first? The boy's mind moved back through time to a still earlier folk. Ah, how cruel it must have been for them in winter, clad in sealskin and otter skin, with only a few shreds of beach-growth to put in their mouths! And yet they had endured till the light's return. How wonderful it must have been to those shadowy folk, the sun of early summer, the springing grass, larksong, the silver legions of fish . . .

Right on the ness stood the ruins of a little medieval monastery.

The boy thought he might just get there before the sun went down. Then he could find his way home well enough in the sunset afterglow.

How tired he was! Here and there, the chapel walls were almost at ground level, but the apse and stone floor of the nave were still there, and a single arch in the south.

About a dozen monks had lived there, the teacher had told him, and the brothers had farmed, fished, kept bees, and recited or sung the 'office' that was appropriate to each season of the turning year.

As the boy set against a gray-lichened wall near the ruined floor, he heard them singing. The separate voices, high and low, grave yet full of joy, interwove, mingled, blended.

There issued from the invisible choir a texture of peace deeper than any natural silence. The hymn was in a foreign language – Norwegian? Gaelic? –– and yet the boy seemed to grasp a meaning at once.

Benedictus es, qui ambulas
super pennas ventorum, super
undas maris. Et laudabilis,
et gloriousus in secula . . .

The sun was down. The first wind of night began to stir, and it shifted a thin wash of sea over the shore stones below, again and again.

The voices in the choir mingled with the wind and the sea and were lost . . .

★   ★   ★

Ah, there was the lamp in the window!

The boy ran up the last slope to the door.

A rich, spicy smell met him at the threshold. The woman – his mother – had baked a large cake.

There it stood on the table, cooling on a wire tray.

The man – his father – was not long in from the sea. A basket of haddocks stood at the door. The fisherman was testing the edge of a knife on his thumb.

'I'm glad you're home,' said the woman. 'There's going to be another storm.'

The wind was beginning to make songs in the chimney.

The boy could hear, through the open door, the noise of the breakers against the stones.

The cow lowed from the byre.

The Old Man in the Snow

'Old Josiah, he's fallen in the snow,' said James, who was six.

They had finished the soup, and Mrs Torvald was putting meat and tatties on the soup-stained plates (to save washing-up).

'Who?' said James' father, John Torvald, the village joiner. 'Somebody's fallen in the snow?'

James said, 'I don't want beef and tatties. I want an orange' . . . In a higher voice he said, 'Josiah fell in the snow.'

'Josiah of Sheepfold?' asked his mother. 'Josiah Smith.'

Grandma stirred the peats in the stove. 'I'm not surprised,' she said. 'Not one bit. It's a wonder he hasn't fallen down dead long ago. An old man like him, going to the pub three or four times a week! He spends all his pension money on drink.'

Mrs Torvald, James' mother, paused, the sauce bottle in her hand.

'How do you know Josiah fell in the snow?' she said.

James' three brothers and two sisters looked at him, curiously and coldly.

'An orange!' cried James. 'I want an orange!'

'Josiah's gone to the dogs since poor Bella died in the spring,'

132

said Grandma. 'Just a cup of tea for me and a biscuit.'

'That boy's a little liar,' said Vera, the oldest of the children. 'How could he have seen Josiah falling in the snow? He's been playing snakes-and-ladders all morning up in the attic, all by himself.'

'No,' said Eric, who was twelve, 'I saw James at the shop an hour ago.'

'No, you never did,' said James. 'I was watching the sheep in the snow.'

'The little liar!' cried Vera.

Robert, who was eight, hit Vera with his wooden spoon. 'James isn't a liar,' he said, 'he's a good boy.'

'All this fighting and argufying!' cried Grandma. 'Them kids, they're wearing my life away. And this Christmas eve.'

'This is serious,' said John Torvald. 'If old Josiah's lying in a snowdrift, he could be dead by now.'

'Frozen to death!' said Vera in a thrilling whisper. 'A hump in the snow.'

'Look here,' said Mrs Torvald to James. 'See here, my lad, Santa won't come near you tonight, till you tell us about Josiah. How do you know he's fallen in the snow?'

James began to cry; at first softly, then in a torrent of sobs, a crescendo, as if his heart would break.

'The lamb!' cried Grandma. 'Look what you've done to him now! He's a good boy. Aren't you a good boy, James? You never tell lies.'

'No,' wailed James, in a last spasm of grief. He bored his knuckles into his eyes. He gave a last snivel or two. Then he sat up in his chair, grave and silent.

'Josiah of Sheepfold fell in the snow.'

'Where?' said his father. 'Where did he fall in the snow?'

James shook his head.

'The pet,' said Grandma. 'He doesn't know one part of the

island from another. Snow looks the same wherever it is. An old small creature like that Josiah, he could fall through the snow like a bird and never be seen.'

'This is very serious, if it's true,' said John Torvald. 'I'll go and have a look before it's dark.'

'I'll come too,' said the two oldest boys, almost together.

The meal ended in a whirl of excitement. Everybody was agitated except James.

'That old fool!' said Grandma. 'Him and his whisky! I knew he would come to a bad end.'

'Will you be lighting the Christmas tree soon?' said James.

Instead of opening his workshop, John Torvald set out for Josiah's cottage on the side of the hill, two miles away.

No use taking the car; the snow-plough hadn't yet cleared the road.

After he left the road and set foot on the hill, it was heavy going. Sometimes John Torvald was up to his knees in unsullied snow.

When he got to Josiah's cottage, there was no one at home and the fire was out. There was a piece of toast and a tea-stained mug on the table.

It had never been a tidy house, but it was a cheerful enough place with the stove burning and Josiah sitting in the rocking-chair with his book and pipe.

Today it seemed like the inside of a neolithic tomb (but for the treasures of skull and broken beaker).

John Torvald walked around the croft and outhouses – a white silence everywhere.

On his way to the pub, John Torvald probed with his eye and stick every slight irregularity in the ditch. Nothing – the snow gave up a rusty petrol can, a bicycle frame, a sheep that rose startled out of its fugitive grave and went wallowing and bleating to join the flock, bright crusts and crumbs falling from its fleece.

'Yes,' said Mr Graham the innkeeper, 'Josiah was here at opening time, 11 o'clock sharp. He left about half past 12.'

'Was he sober?' asked John Torvald.

'Sober enough,' said Mr Graham. 'Let me see. He had his usual, two nips of whisky and two glasses of beer. I think one or two of the boys stood him a dram, seeing it's Christmas.'

Half-a-dozen heads at the bar counter looked up from draughts and dominoes, and were slowly and solemnly shaken.

'Is there something the matter with him?' asked Mr Graham.

'He never got home,' said John Torvald. 'He was seen falling in a snowdrift.'

'Where?'

'That I don't know.'

There was a certain amount of concern in the inn. Most of the men liked Josiah, although he was a bit of a cadger, and in drink, sometimes an intolerable bore with his stories of sea-going and whaling and all the sweethearts he had had in his youth here and there, in the islands and beyond.

'Maybe he has a new lady-friend,' said Frank the young fisherman.

'He was very gray in the face this morning,' said the farmer of Quoys. 'I didn't like the look of him.'

It's not a good day for an old man to collapse in the snow,' said Sam Scott the blacksmith.

They agreed, shaking their heads. That would be about the worst thing that could happen to a frail old body, in the depths of winter.

Draughts players and domino players gathered round John Torvald at the end of the bar.

Mr Graham the innkeeper was so perturbed that he had forgotten to shout 'Time, gentlemen!' at 2.30. Constable Robert

Sweyn, tall and blue-black, was suddenly there, in the door.

Half-a-dozen voices told the policeman about Josiah, confusedly. He held up his hand for silence. John Torvald told him the simple facts.

Constable Sweyn removed his cap and scratched his head. At last he said, 'A search party. A search party will have to be formed.'

By this time word had got round the village. There was quite a gathering of folk outside the inn door. Children and dogs came running with smoking breath from the far end of the village and the nearer crofts.

'Old Josiah's lost!' That was the word in every mouth.

Most of the growing assembly looked pleased and excited. A few heads were shaken, gravely.

Dogs barked from distant farms – the sound came shivering across the snow.

Constable Sweyn said, 'It'll be dark in an hour. We'll have to hurry. No use after sunset. He'll be dead. The frost'll get to his heart.'

The doctor's car drew up. Dr Silver was informed of the affair. 'Yes, indeed,' he said, 'it could be very serious. The search should start right away.'

'I was about to organise a few small search-parties,' said Constable Sweyn.

The minister came from the manse and stood outside the inn for the first time in his life. 'A good man, Josiah,' he said, 'a very good old man.'

Women stood in doors here and there. Some of the old women were shawled; they shook their heads. Grandma was at the door of the Torvald house. She shook her head longer than the others; as if to say, 'I knew it would come to this!'

Meantime Constable Sweyn was forming search-parties of three or four – each party to search a different part of the island. The blacksmith led one group, the farmer of Quoys another,

Frank the fisherman a third, John Torvald the fourth and last.

'We'll need to hurry,' said Constable Sweyn.

Bonneted, quilted, scarfed to the mouths, with sticks and dogs the search-parties fanned out over the island. Children danced in the rear and pelted each other with snowballs; like bells the crystal echoes of their laughter fell among the valleys and frozen waters.

'Be silent!' cried Constable Sweyn. 'This is a serious business ...'

After that, for a while, the children – including four young Torvalds – contented themselves with giggling into their mittens.

'There's something!' cried Willie Olaf, aged eleven, pointing at an irregularity under the snow, a hidden hieroglyph. It turned out to be a piece of sacking.

Indeed they would need to hurry. Already the little Christmas trees were displaying their magical multi-coloured fruits in this window and that.

The sun was low in the west, coated in crimson. The tranquil ocean blazed like stained glass.

The four search parties called to each other from time to time: thin shivering cries. 'No luck ...' 'Nothing doing ...'

'I've found him! Here he is, up against the wall here, at the Glebe!'

The cry brought them all together, stumbling and floundering through the snow. Sounds of harsh breath only – the children came behind, intent, rising and falling, with smoking breaths.

It turned out to be a scarecrow that the farmer of Glebe had thrown into the ditch, after ten summers of corn-keeping. His snow-mound was rudely disturbed.

How the children laughed! They melled, they collided, they fell about in the snow. That old Josiah Smith should be mistaken for a scarecrow!

'Get home, you kids!' cried Mr Graham of the inn. 'You're

just a nuisance. You're in everybody's way.'

The children retreated silently to the wall of the Glebe barn.

The scarecrow was returned to his dazzling grave.

And now a flush of rose went over the island. The sun was down. The first stars were out. Diamond points of frost glittered on fencing post, telegraph line, hen-house.

The sea westward was a glooming mirror. Shadows began to fill up the island hollows and valleys.

The groups dispersed again. A few had been wise enough to bring torches. There were random flashes here and there. They cried with voices brittle as glass: 'Nothing doing ...' 'It's getting too dark ...'

Clearly it was too late. Constable Sweyn shouted, 'Everybody come to the crossroads! Stop the search!'

At the crossroads. Dr Silver said, 'Let's get this clear. I understand that a child saw Josiah falling in a drift. If we knew *where,* roughly, that would make our job easier.'

John Torvald said, 'It was James – my boy – he's only six. He saw it happening, but he won't say where.'

'We ought to go and have a word with young James,' said the minister.

They went, a darkling troop, to the Torvald house. John Torvald ushered them inside to the fire. Mrs Torvald put the kettle on the stove, to make tea.

The children yelled outside, under the stars. Another snow battle had begun.

James was asleep in his little bed in the corner. A thick white rubber-boot stocking hung at the foot of the bed; waiting for midnight and Santa.

The Christmas tree stood in the corner; it was out of a Scandinavian forest of coloured enchantment.

'No,' said Mrs Torvald. 'I'm sorry, but I won't wake him. I've had enough trouble getting him off to sleep, with all this

Christmas excitement. He's told us all that he can tell us. Now, who takes sugar in their tea?'

'It would give James a terrible fright, right enough,' said the blacksmith, 'if he was to wake up and see twenty ugly faces round his bed.'

James slept on; the breath coming sweet and soft and regular. He smelt of apples and dew.

There James lay, drifted under poppy-leaves; he kept his secret.

'That poor old man,' said Grandma from the fireside chair, 'to think of him lying stiff and stark out there. Ah, it would have been a good thing if Bella had been spared and he had been taken! Whisky, wanderings here and there across the face of the globe, fancy-women. The wonder is, Bella put up with him so long.'

Solemnly the searchers drank their tea. They shuffled their feet. One by one they put down their cups.

'I suppose,' said the blacksmith, 'what we ought to do now is knock on every door in the island. It would do no good. He never visited anybody. And nobody would let him in over their threshold.'

Mr Graham looked at his watch. 'Ten to five,' he said, 'I must be getting back. Time to open the bar.'

'Thank you, Mrs Torvald, for your hospitality,' said the minister. 'I hope this most joyous night of the year won't be marred by tragedy.'

'Alas,' said Grandma. 'Alas!'

One by one the searchers passed out into the night. The snow smashed like frail glass under their boots. It had begun to freeze hard.

At midnight all the children were in bed, and so was Grandma; and Mrs Torvald had just gone, having stuffed the Christmas goose with oatmeal and herbs.

John Torvald went outside, to see that all was well in the village, as he always did before going to bed.

At Sheepfold there was a lamp in the window: a frail daffodil light on the ridge between the stars and the snow.

He was too tired to trek the two miles to Sheepfold again.

He would go in the morning.

'Fall in the snow?' said Josiah. 'Coming home from the pub I fell in the snow. I slipped on ice, and head over heels I went into a drift of snow. I tried to get up but I couldn't. Do you know this? After a time I began to enjoy it, lying there happed up in snow. I began to feel sleepy and contented. *Well*, says I to myself, *this* is it, *Josiah, this is journey's end, you're nearly home. No more rheumatics, no more loneliness and hangovers – nothing. Dying's fine and easy. Why are folk so scared of it?*

And do you know this, John, I turned and pulled more snow over me like a quilt? And I felt as happy as a cat at fire … I opened my eyes once, and there was a very small boy standing on the road looking down at me. He just looked at me for a while, very serious, and went away.'

'That was James, my youngest,' said John Torvald.

'I thought about that boy,' said Josiah. 'I thought about ships and seaports, music and fights and ale, all the happy times that boy had before him. Stars and snow and cornfields. And girls, sweethearts – especially them. I felt good, lying there remembering sweethearts. What a good way to slip into the silence, I thought, remembering Maggie and Cilia, Juanita and Hilde, and old Bella … Then I suddenly remembered something – I had an appointment that afternoon with Sarah Strom over at Scad – you know her, Sarah, a widow woman. Sarah had asked me to Scad that same afternoon for my tea. She would be putting the kettle on! A Christmas cake would be on the table. My present would be on the mantle-piece, wrapped in fancy paper ... I'm telling you, John, it was a great effort for me to drag myself out of that wave of snow. It had all but drowned me. But I got on my feet. I must have looked like a winter ghost as I hobbled across the hill to Sarah's. Pooh! I soon dried out at Sarah's fire. And she gave me a dram. And then we had tea and Christmas cake. And I smoked a pipe. And I got home just as the old clock on the mantle-piece was striking midnight.'

John Torvald told him about the search-party, the alarms and excursions of the hour before sundown.

'I thought I heard shouts in the hill, indeed,' said Josiah, 'when Sarah and me were at our tea. I thought it was a few drunks. John, tell me this, do you think I'm too old to take another wife? I'm lonely here at Sheepfold. And Sarah and me might get on well enough for a winter or two yet.'

John said that in his opinion nobody was too old for happiness.

'I'm glad to hear you say that,' said Josiah. 'I've had so many sweethearts, I think I must have had more than my share. Your mother, John, she was a sweetheart of mine a whole summer, between two voyages. A good woman. Tell her I'm asking for her.'

John Torvald got to his feet. 'I hope you have no ill effects from falling in the snow, Josiah,' he said.

'Nothing that a dram won't cure,' said Josiah. 'I'm very thankful to that boy of yours — James, is it? If James hadn't seen me falling in the drift, I wouldn't be sitting beside this fire now. James led me back to the land of the living.'

At the door John Torvald said, 'Where exactly did you fall into the snow?'

The old man shook his head. 'There was whiteness every-where,' he said. 'My eyes were dazzled.'

They had a Christmas dram together from the bottle John Torvald took out of his coat pocket.

Darkness and Light

Hogmanay – what did it bring but wind, and rain, and after dark whirls of snow that melted as soon as it fell, except in certain sheltered places and in folds of the hills? And then, towards midnight, rain again, long wind-spun drenching ropes of wetness.

There was no light in Ben's house above the shore. Most likely he had gone to bed. What had Ben to rejoice about? Sanna had been in the kirkyard since early November. Mockery it had been after all, twelve months ago, when the first-footers stood about Ben and Sanna's fire and said, in their dark and bright hogmanay voices, 'Happy New Year!' . . . 'Health and prosperity to Ben and Sanna!' Then the mingled tinklings of glass and pouring whisky.

Early on New Year morning the coat of rain was torn from the island sky. A few stars appeared, in the north and the west. The road glittered here and there with pool-stars, ditch-stars, stone-stars. A voice sounded from this house and that: figures appeared in doorways, shrugging into coats, the doorways were rich lighted rectangles in the solid block of this farm, that croft. Torches flickered and beamed: shadows trooped into one company of hearty shadows at the end of a road. More and more stars enriched the sky. They were bright enough, the stars, to put a gleam on tilted bottles, to invest a winter ditch with minute jewellery.

'Where'll we go first?' came a voice from the troop of shadows.

'To Crufdale, of course,' came the response (a high heroic voice). 'To Ben's and Sanna's.'

This was followed by a brief silence, a shuffling of feet. Someone coughed.

'To Ben's,' said a low voice. 'We'll go to Ben's now. . . .'

At Crufdale the door was locked. The place was in blackness, or almost in blackness: when Tommy put his forge-red face against the window, there was a glow in the grate. In the deep chair beside the grate sat Ben. Ben's eyes shone in a sudden flare and gulp of flame from the banked fire.

'Ben, it's us!' cried Tommy. 'Let's in, Ben.'

Other voices were at the window then; other breath, that stained the glass so that Ben was a glimmering ghost inside. 'A Happy New Year, Ben!' And, 'Open up, Ben! We've got some good malt here.' And, 'Are you all right, Ben?'

Ben paid no more attention than if they had been shadows indeed, and voiceless shadows.

'A queer old thing!' said Sander when five fruitless minutes of cajolery and raillery had passed. 'I always told you, he would break up if anything happened to Sanna.'

'It was Sanna we always came to see,' said Geoff. 'Sanna was the cheery one.'

'A queer way to start the year!' said Bilton beside the peatstack. 'Turned away from the first door – an unlucky thing, that!'

From the gate Tommy called back. 'A good year anyway, Ben! May it be a better year for you than the one that's just past.'

They exchanged bottles on the road outside. They heard other revellers a mile away, coming along the hill road: a chorus, a high wild sudden 'yarroo!' as if a Cherokee had been enrolled in their company.

The rejected first-footers set off to the hamlet that straggled along the shore a mile to the north, a scatter of bright and dark windows.

The night put on its rain-coat again and the dozen companies of first-footers were soaked, all over the island. To some the rain was a delicious sky-essence dripping from their noses, breaking up their vision comically, filling the road with beautiful brimming mirrors that their feet smashed uncertainly through, time and again. To others the rain was the last twist in their rack of misery. It rained from four o'clock in the morning till after six, a wind-wavering downpour, a lustration upon the door-step of the new year. Then the rain-coat was torn again, and the first star shone through.

In the last of the rain Amos came to Ben's door. His pocket bulged with a dark load. He lifted the latch and pushed. The door rattled but remained fast.

'Ben!' shouted Amos. 'Are you in your bed, man? It's me, Amos.' The house was silent as a stone.

Amos took his face to the window. There, over the fire-glow, crouched Ben. Amos knocked sharply on the pane. Ben didn't let on to hear. As Amos watched, Ben took a cup from the hearth and put the rim to his mouth and tilted it. Whisky gives the face of the drinker a different expression from tea or ale or water.

'Ben,' shouted Amos, and knocked again.

At a distant farm a dog barked wildly, and was as suddenly silent. Another household was receiving those who carried the New Year blessing.

And now Amos saw that Ben was speaking and probably

speaking to him; for the eyes of the old boatman were fixed on him. The mouth moved, the old hands gesticulated a little, the head nodded gently from time to time.

'I can't hear you, man,' shouted Amos. 'Let me in! I thought you might be lonely. That's why I came.'

It seemed to Amos that Ben smiled from time to time. But he made no move to stir from armchair to door, to let his oldest friend in. He opened his palm in Amos's direction, his mouth moved, his eyes crinkled again. There was a brief silence; he shook his head; then he resumed the inaudible monologue.

Amos brought the whisky bottle out of his pocket and held it up. That might be the key that would let him in. It turned out not to be. Through the glass Ben continued to talk to Amos mildly and reasonably.

Nothing is more infuriating than a seen language that is incomprehensible: a cry under water, a shout into a gale. What was the one old man trying to tell the other? Maybe that this Hogmanay business was a lot of nonsense – hordes of young drunken yahoos – their last year's greetings and kissings hadn't done Sanna much good. . . . He could have been saying, on the other hand, that the rowan tree at the end of the house had been loaded with berries and so it was likely to be a hard winter; he hoped Amos has plenty of peats in his stack.

Was he trying to tell Amos that a letter had come at last from young Ben in Alberta. But there was nothing of importance in the letter, the usual items of getting and spending – nothing important enough, at any rate, to make him rise from his comfortable chair.

It was possible that Ben was speaking about Sanna. It seemed likely, indeed, from the frequent smiles that dimpled the soliloquy. They had been as happy together, give and take a few fights, rows, sulks and silences, as any couple in the island. He was telling Amos maybe that yes – it was lonely now without

Sanna. Why on earth was Sanna taken and Ben left that could do hardly a thing for himself? (The district nurse had to see to him once a week. The home-help came weekly, too, to clean up his dust and bruck.)

Could Ben be saying – what was true – that Amos had courted Sanna the summer before Ben himself had appeared on the scene, newly home from sea after a year's sailing? Though Ben had married Sanna the next spring, for some reason Ben had always seemed to be jealous that Amos had got the first of Sanna's kisses; and for that reason, it could be, he wasn't letting Amos in on this particular night. Let him bide out there in the darkness and the rain. It was Sanna Amos had always really come to see at New Year. Why couldn't he go down to the kirkyard and talk to Sanna there?

That, thought Amos (his hands and eyes soaked with another blind shower) would be a likely thing for Ben to say. He might indeed visit Sanna in the kirkyard before going home to his porridge and tea.

Amos, stone deaf in the last of the rain and the darkness, shook his head and stamped his feet. Once he opened his bottle and threw his head back and let his Adam's apple wobble. He sprinkled a few drops of whisky over the window-sill. 'A good year to this house anyway,' he said.

Inside, Ben poked the fire. He took another small sip out of the cup on the hearth. He turned to the patient man at the window; smiling; nodding; crinkling his eyes; moving his mouth into a hundred shapes.

It could have been great wisdom or great poetry, though that was unlikely, coming from Ben.

'I expect,' thought Amos, 'he's wishing me luck, among other things, with the croft this coming year – a good sowing and harvest. He's a kind man, Ben, though he was always a bit lazy himself, as far as the fishing went. Sanna didn't exactly live like a duchess.'

When Amos, after his solitary toast and blessing, turned to go home, the winter sun was just rising in the south-east. The new light brightened his forehead. Behind him, Ben's window flashed and flamed.

The Winter Song

At graystones I got nothing. They were all in bed. Darkness. I sang outside, under a dark blue coat of sky with three stars in it.

> Good to be this buirdly bigging!
> We're a' St Mary's men.
> Fae the steeth-stane to the rigging
> Afore wur Lady.

They slept the year out, good temperance people.

At the old ones', Jonah's and Jess's, I got a glass of ginger beer and a penny. I put my mouth in this shape and that.

> God bless the gudewife and sae the gudeman
> We're a' St Mary's men
> Dish and table, pot and pan
> Afore wur Lady.

They clapped their hands. Old Jess kissed me. The row of blue dishes twinkled on the sideboard.

At Peggy's, no luck. Her door was locked. Peggy was visiting Jock her sweetheart. I sang a verse for the house, all the same, under a purple one-star robe of sky.

> Where is the gudewife o' this hoose?
> Where is she, that dame?

At Mirran and Tom's, Mirran shook a finger at me. 'Why aren't you with the other boys? I swear, you're the strangest loneliest boy in this island.' I sang a verse, my voice shaking. Mirran has a sharp tongue.

> Gudeman, go to your brewing vat
> And fetch us here a quart o' that

Mirran gave me the thickest piece of gingerbread I had ever blocked my mouth on. The magic of winter was in that gingerbread. It glowed in my belly. 'Well sung,' said Tom. Mirran pinched her thin face into a smile.

At Tofthouse, the dog set up, when I'd knocked, the blackest barking! Nobody opened the door. There had been a death in that place in November: Rachel who made the butter and lit the fires.

> Whar is the servant lass o' this hoose?
> Whar is she, that lass?

I set my small song against the black mouth of Faithful the dog.

At old Sillock's, sixpence – it shone between my fingers like a star! Two verses I gave the grey fisherman.

King Henry he is no at hame
But he is to the greenwids gane

He had taken the coin from a bottle at the back of the bed, like an old pirate king who has been in far perilous places and gives rich rewards.

At Billtock's, nothing. Billtock had been taken away to the poor-house after harvest. Now a stone has fallen from the roof. I whispered a few words of the song into the rusty keyhole.

May a' your hens rin in a reel,
And every ane twal' at her heel

Son of Billtock, come back soon from Australia. The heart of the house is, now, a cold black hearth. The hen-house is a cluster of wet boards.

At Nessvoe, Willie and Jessie set me in their great straw chair, legs dangling. Willie looked at me solemnly through owl spectacles (price one shilling from the wandering hawker). Jessie gave me a cup of ale. I sang till the cups on Jessie's dresser shivered. The ale had made me reckless and gay. I uttered all kinds of blessing, half the song.

May a' your kye be weel to calf
And every ane hae a queyo calf
May a' your mares be weel to foal
And every ane hae a mare foal
May a' your yowes be weel to lamb
And every ane hae a yowe and a ram . . .

'That's not likely,' said Willie, and he eyed me like a friendly owl.

150

At the sea-captain's, nothing. 'Impudent little wretch! Begging, is it? Does your mother know you're out in the dark night begging? A disgrace. That nonsense of a song, January after January – I'm sick of it! . . . Go away, boy. I'm poor. I have nothing for you. I've navigated a hundred seas to come home and get some peace at last. I don't have sovereigns in a teapot under the stair – all lies, nonsense. Impudent little pirate that you are . . . That wind's blowing off Iceland. You best hurry off home, pirate. There's a gale and a blizzard coming.'

> We hae wur ships sailan the sea
> And mighty men o' lands are we

I sang to the wharf-bound miserable rotting hulk of a house.

Andrew and Annie are just newly married in a new house, Rosevale. I sang,

> This night is good New 'ar ev'n's night
> And we've come here to claim wur right
> Goodwife, go to your butter ark
> And weigh us oot o' that ten mark

Andrew and Annie laughed. 'A bairn's blessing on a new fire and bed – what better?' They gave me what was left of the wedding largesse, the squandered 'boys ba' ' – one penny and four ha' pennies and three farthings. I stayed so long at their leaping fire, the load of money in my pocket burned through to my thigh. Annie bade me 'A Good New Year!' Her voice rang like a bell under the frosty lintel.

On the hillside, a star or a snowflake fell cold on my nose. I heard, on the far side of the hill, the horde of village boys going with their threatening chorus.

> Be ye maids or be ye nane
> Ye's a' be kissed or we gang hame
> If you dunno open your door
> We'll lay it flat upon the floor

'I hope they don't meet me!' Silver moths fell and folded on my shivering cheek and fingers.

At Norbreck, nothing. Sander lives alone. He's deaf. He goes to bed early. What good's a song to a deaf widowed wall-facer? I sang. Flakes fluttered on to his window, a silver host.

> If we get no what we seek
> We'll tak' the head o' your Yule sheep

Sander slept, dreaming of flocks and a bonny fireside spinner long dust.

Near the Glebe, I fell in the ditch. The singing horde of boys went past, with flake-dark lanterns, a field away. I sang, all slush and blue bruises, to the twelve whisky drinkers in the Glebe. One of them offered me his flask. I filled my mouth with flames and glory and the richness of furrows.

> And the three-legged cog that's standing fu'
> Fetch it here to weet wur mou'

> This is the best that we can tak'
> And we will drink till wur lugs crack

A fiddle struck up. An eightsome reel went round, with Cherokee yells.

★   ★   ★

I stood, a boy of stars, at the laird's gate. The gentry did not hear me. Inside, bunches of candles, broken ceiling lights from a bell made of crystal pieces that collided and made tiny music. Mirrors glooming and softly gleaming. Mr Sweyn the laird would be nodding in his oak chair between the flames and the decanter. His silver-haired lady sat opposite sewing an alphabet on a sampler. They do not hear a small fist on the mighty ancient door panels of the Hall.

> Good be tae this buirdly bigging
> We're a' St Mary's men
> Fae the steethe-stane tae the rigging
> Afore wur Lady

Hall or hovel, don't the doors and windows and chimneys need as much blessing as they can get, always? 'We're poor things, even at the best,' my grandfather would say, sadly and wonderingly, when word would come to the island of the death of a prince or a millionaire.

My pocket rang like a bell, going shorewards. I heaved home, a pirate ship blizzard-borne between black sky and eerie-white glimmering earth. I dipped home with a cargo of coins and stars.

And my mother cried in the open door, 'Where have you been? What a sight, filth from eyes to feet! Snow in your hair! Your supper's cold' . . . The baby cried from the cradle. Granda nodded over by the fire. Stars whirled past my shoulder on to the blue stone floor. My mother put a kiss on my cheek, a sweet red warm star. Granda, sipping his Hogmanay toddy, grumbled at a sudden blown star-swirling coldness upon the knees and hands of his last winter.

My mother closed the door. Our fire flamed like the sun. I ate a hot buttered bannock. The croft was a little secure summer in the heart of perpetual snow. My mother sang to the child. I nodded off to sleep, my head like a bee-hive.

A Croft in January

'You stay indoors,' said the boy's mother, a new widow. 'Sit over there beside the fire. Read a book. This is the most treacherous time of the year, January. I don't want any more illness in this house I'll put another peat on the fire. There's a good boy. I'll just be back from the byre.'

As soon as his mother went to milk the cow, the boy was out and away.

Oh, it was bleak all right! The Hogmanay snow was shrinking. It had been beautiful while it lay like a white quilt over the island, under the full moon. But now the snow had shrunk to tattered rags of grey along the dykes and on the hill-top.

As he came round the corner, the wind cut into him like a scythe.

He ran towards the village. The melting snow on the road seeped into his boots and he felt his feet cold. Thin spits of rain came out of the grey sky . . . This was better, though, than the grief and the silence of the fatherless croft.

In the first days after New Year – after the first-footing and the whisky bottles and the singing of the old midwinter song in every croft – the village seemed always to shrink into itself and batten down for the worst of winter. For, as the old folk said, 'as the day lengthens the caald strengthens' . . .

The length of the village, there was nobody to be seen. The boy peeked in at the inn door. The fire was burning for nobody. John Baillie the inn-keeper was playing patience on the dry counter. Where, this afternoon, were all the merry men of recent days, with their red faces and loud mouths and bottles of whisky sticking out of their pockets? Where were the miller, the blacksmith, the three fishermen, the seven crofters, the shepherd, the ferryman? They were crouched, wretched and penniless, over the fires here and there – and the tongues of womenfolk making their hangovers more wretched.

The thought of his father came to the boy. Well, he was beyond songs and ale-house fires and hangovers now. And his mother was more silent than ever she had been, except when she broke out in complainings.

'Your brother should be here, him that emigrated to Australia ten years ago. Your father might have died quiet then. This croft has been in the one family for seven generations. The way things are, it's the poor-house for you and me, boy. I don't want their charity. There was Willa of Taing here last night when you were sleeping, with eggs and oat-cakes. I sent her about her business.'

The sun was down. He saw the postman going with his lantern and bag across the hill.

He had one penny in his pocket. Oh, he was glad to see that the shop was open. It had been closed since Hogmanay.

He went inside. Sandra, the general merchant, had no customers either. She looked up from her fair-isle knitting. 'A pennyworth of pandrops,' said the boy.

'You're all blue and shivering,' said Sandra. 'It's no weather for a boy like you to be out. I'm surprised your mother let you over the door.'

She tilted a white rattling rush of pandrops from the jar on the counter into a white paper poke.

'It'll be a poor year up at Svendale, this,' said Sandra. 'I think a pity of your poor mother. Who's going to plough your field this February? It's a hard thing when the bread-winner's taken.'

Sandra put the poke of sweeties on the counter. The boy put his last penny on the counter.

'No no,' said Sandra. 'You keep your penny. This is a present for you.'

'I don't want charity,' said the boy. He picked up the sweetie-bag and left the shop.

'Always a proud lot up at Svendale,' he heard the old shop-wife saying as the door pinged behind him.

The village lay like a grey corpse under the first darkness. A star flickered like a candle between two urgent clouds.

The boy had never known such desolation. The year was dead, the village was dead, the shutters of destitution would be nailed across the windows of their croft in the month of May, when there was no money to meet the rent.

Ah, there was a third lighted door in the village! Willie Learmonth the fisherman was alive, thank goodness.

The pools along the village street were beginning to freeze over. He almost slipped and fell, crossing over to the boat-shed above the shore. He opened Willie's door without knocking. Willie was sitting over by the stove baiting his lines beside the paraffin lamp. 'If it isn't Thorfinn!' he cried. 'A happy New Year, Thorfinn. Come over by the stove and warm you.'

'Where's Tom and Andrew?' said the boy.

'They're still recovering from Hogmanay,' said the fisherman. 'Somebody must work. So here I am. I have no wife to rage at me, I'm thankful to say.'

'Please, Willie,' said the boy, 'I'd be very pleased if you'd sign me on soon. I've always wanted to be a fisherman with you on the *Venture*. I don't like farming.'

Willie the fisherman eyed him gravely. 'Well,' said he, 'maybe after summer – or the spring after that. You need a bit more muscle and bone on you. I'll be glad for you to be on the *Venture* then.'

'I see,' said the boy.

'Look,' said Willie. 'I have some salted ling in the rafters. Take some home to your mother. Wish her, from me, a better year than she had last year, poor soul.'

'We don't take charity,' said the boy.

When the boy got home, slithering on the ice, he expected no less a tongue-lashing than the hung-over New Year celebrants had gotten from their woman-folk on January the second.

But his mother was in her chair with the lamp-light on her face and a paper in her hand. The postman had called. 'A letter from your brother in Australia. Fancy that, after ten years! A sheep farmer, that's what he is. And look at this!' . . . He read, by the firelight, a postal draft for ten pounds.

'This'll pay the rent and plenty to spare,' said his mother. 'We can keep the cow. I can even buy two sheep and a flock of hens. Our furniture won't be set on the road outside, in May. Some folk will be disappointed, I dare say.'

'I have news too,' said the boy. 'Willie Learmonth of the *Venture* is taking me on for a fisherman.'

An Epiphany Tale

There was once a small boy and he was deaf and dumb and blind.

He knew nothing about Christmas. All he knew was that it got cold at a certain time of the year. He would touch a stone with his fingers. His fingers burned with frost!

One day the boy was sitting on his mother's doorstep wrapped in a thick coat and scarf against the cold.

A stranger came and stood above him. There was a good smell from the stranger's hands and beard. It was different from the smell of the village people; the fishermen and the shepherds and their women and children and animals. The man smelt of sunrise.

The stranger touched the boy's ear. At once he could hear all the village sounds – the sea on the stones, his mother at the hearth baking scones, the seagulls, and the children playing in the field.

'No,' his mother was saying to the stranger, 'I don't want to buy a pan or a fork from your pack. No use speaking to the boy – he's deaf as a stone. Look, I'll give you a scone to eat. We're poor. I have no money to buy a thing.'

The boy didn't understand what the stranger and his mother said. The interchange of sounds seemed to him to be more wonderful than anything he could ever have imagined, and the most wonderful was the stranger's voice.

It said, 'Thank you for the bread, woman.'

Soon the stranger was no longer there. He had taken his rich silk smell and his clanging treasure away. The boy sat on the doorstep as the multitudinous harp of the world was stroked again and again. His mother kneaded dough on the board and stoked the peat fire.

Then the doors of his ears were closed once more. He laughed, silently.

★　★　★

Another smell drifted across the boy's nostrils, different from anything he had known. It was like incense of darkness, a circling of bright swift animals.

The second stranger touched the boy's eyes. They opened. The things he saw all at once amazed him with their beauty and variety. A few flakes of snow were falling on the dead ditch-grass. Gray clouds huddled along the sky. A cat crossed the road from a fishing-boat below with a small fish in its mouth.

Two people were arguing in the door. The white strenuous kind face must be his mother's. The black smiling face belonged to the stranger. Both were beautiful.

The boy's looked into the gloom of the house. The flames in the hearth were so beautiful it gave him a catch in the breath.

Clearly his mother was refusing to have anything to do with the objects the stranger was spreading out before her: soft shining fabrics, ivory combs, a few sheets with music and poems on them. The boy did not know what they were – each was marvellous and delightful in its different way.

At last his mother, exasperated, took a fish that had been smoking in the chimney. She gave it to the black man. He smiled. He tied up his pack. He turned to the boy and raised his hand in a gesture of farewell.

The boy's mother shook her head: as if to say, 'There's no point in making signs to this poor child of mine. He's been as blind as a worm from the day he was born.'

Then, to her amazement, the boy raised a blue wintry hand, and smiled and nodded farewell to the second stranger.

For an hour the boy's eyes gazed deep into the slowly-turning sapphire of the day. His mother moving between fire and board; the three fishermen handing a basket of fish from the stern of their boat to half-a-dozen shore-fast women; the gulls wheeling above; the thickening drift of flakes across the village chimneys; a boy and a girl throwing snowballs at each other — all were dances more beautiful than he could have imagined.

Then the luminous stone dulled and flawed. Between one bread dance and another, while his mother stood and wiped her flame-flushed brow at the window, she became a shadow. The boy was as sightless as he had ever been. He laughed, silently.

★   ★   ★

It was the most wonderful day the boy had ever known. And still the day wasn't over.

He was aware of a third presence at the door, lingering. This stranger brought with him smells of green ice, flashing stars, seal-pelts.

The mother, at her wits' end now, mixed with those smells of the pole her own smells of flour and butter and peat-smoke. The boy knew that his mother was angry; the smells came from her in fierce thrusting swirls.

It was enough to drive the most importunate pedlar away, but the man from the far north stood mildly at the threshold.

161

The boy could imagine a bland quiet smile.

His mother's anger never lasted long. Another smell came to the boy's quivering nostrils: ale. His mother had poured a bottle of ale for the stranger, to refresh him for his journey. And now the smells of ice and fire and malt mingled gently in the doorway.

'I wonder,' thought the boy, 'what they're saying to each other? The same beautiful things as before, I expect. Their hands and their mouths will be making the same good shapes.'

It seemed a marvel to him that his ears and his eyes had been opened both in one day. How could any human being endure such ravishment of the senses, every hour of every day for many winters and summers?

The winter sun was down. The boy felt the first shadow on the back of his hand.

It was the time now for all the villagers to go indoors for the night. But this day they didn't go straight home. The fishermen and their wives and children came and lingered on the road outside the boy's door. He could smell the sweet milk breath of the children, and the sea breath of the men and the well-and–peat breath of the women. (Also he could smell the ashen breath of one old villager who would, he knew, be dead before the new grass.)

The villagers had come to stare at the stranger. The aroma of malt ebbed slowly. The boy felt the stone shivering; the stranger, having drunk, had put down his pewter mug on the doorstep.

Then he felt the touch of a finger on his locked mouth. He opened it. All his wonder and joy and gratitude for this one festival day gathered to his lips and broke out in a cry.

His mother dropped her baking bowl on the floor, in her astonishment. The bowl broke in a hundred pieces.

The old man who was soon to die said he had heard many rare sounds in his life, but nothing so sweet and pure as the boy's one cry.

The youngest villager was a child in her mother's arms that day. She remembered that sound all her life. Nothing that she heard ever afterwards, a lover's coaxing words, or a lark over a cornfield, or the star of birth that broke from the mouth of her own first child, no utterance seemed to be half as enchanting as the single incomprehensible word of the dumb boy.

Some of the stupider villagers said he had made no sound at all. How could he? – he had never spoken before, he would never utter a word again. A mouse had squeaked in the thatch, perhaps.

The stranger left in the last of the light. He joined two other darkling figures on the ridge.

The villagers dispersed to their houses.

The boy went indoors to the seat beside the fire. How flustered his mother was! What a day she had had! Her baking interrupted by three going-around men – her best blue china bowl in smithereens – her poor boy stricken with wonderment in the shifting net of flame shadows! She had never seen him like this before. He touched his ears, his eyes, his mouth, as if his body was an instrument that he must prepare for some great music.

And yet, poor creature, he was as dumb and deaf and blind as he had ever been.

The boy sat and let the flame-shadows play on him.

The mother washed her floury hands in the basin. Then she crossed the flagstone floor and bent over him and kissed him.

He sat, his stone head laved with hearth flames.

I Saw Three Ships...

'There will be no more Christmas,' cried Cromwell's chaplain. 'Christmas is abolished and forbid in the islands here, as it has been put down everywhere in this commonwealth. We will have no more of such ancient mummery.'

This man in a black coat, Cromwell's chaplain, had a loud voice that could be heard from one end of Kirkwall to the other.

The five soldiers guarding the clergymen struck their mailed hands together. The iron noise might have set your teeth on edge.

'Ought we not to be glad of the Saviour's birth?' said a sailor from the edge of the crowd. 'We have always guised and danced and made good cheer at this time in winter.' 'Yes,' said the chaplain, 'but it was all vain enactment and a riotous brawl in the street over a football, and drunkenness. We have put all that vanity behind us. Celebrate in a seemly way, by reading the Good Book in the peace of your own homes and hearths.' The brewer shouted, 'I have brewed a hundred gallons for Yule. We brew a hundred gallons every Yule, sometimes more.'

A mailed fist was put to the angry mouth of John Fara the

brewer and taverner.

'Say no more, John Fara,' said the old wandering wife that sold pins and spools of thread. 'Say no more, or they'll empty your good Yule ale down the drains.' John Fara went away with a bleeding mouth.

Christmas celebrations or no, the troopers of Cromwell made a great hullabaloo on the longest night, in their tents, singing and fighting and lurching here and there, this way and that. John Fara need not have worried: the soldiers carried away his hogsheads at night and paid in good ringing silver groats.

Cromwell's chaplain slept in a web of sombre dreams.

John Fara thought it worth the loss of a tooth.

John Fara kept an ale-house for-bye brewing, and he had a deep cellar of very ancient good ale that only a few folk had knowledge of.

★   ★   ★

That black chaplain of Cromwell when he passed down the street of Kirkwall, it was as if he wore the snell east wind for a coat.

He had forbid worship in the old cathedral of St Magnus.

It was overheard, what he said to Cromwell's colonel. 'No stables for the horses, sir? There's a fine roomy stable for a score of horses, with fodder and all accoutrements, in the huge kirk here that used to be a cathedral, before the painted maskers called bishops were put down.'

So stalls were put up in the ancient kirk and the horses went in, one after another, and their hooves struck stars from the worn venerated stones.

The provost's house that had been commandeered for a barracks, a large room there was made the meeting-house for prayer and sermon. From there Cromwell's chaplain shepherded the minds and hearts of troopers and townsfolk. He thundered out sermons, an hour long.

But still a few townsfolk and seamen and country folk knew a secret side door into St Magnus that was not known to the Round-heads and there they foregathered on a Sabbath night in mid-winter, and said their prayers in low hushed voices, by the dim lantern-glow.

Certain citizens in the pay of Cromwell indicated the doors of those who did not attend at the meeting-house in the barracks.

Men reckoned that that was the longest coldest dreichest winter ever known in Orkney.

Men had to hide their fiddles and flutes, lest they be confiscated and broken and burned.

*   *   *

Three shepherds came into the town from Wideford and Keelylang. They were such solitary men that they knew only vague rumours of Cromwell and the troopers and the 'purification.' Foreign soldiers were nothing new – the Scots had sent their armed ruffians over the islands two generations ago ... Down into Kirkwall came the shepherds, and went straight to John Fara's ale-house for a round or two of Yule ale.

They passed a man they had never seen before, who was like a black column. Cromwell's chaplain eyed them, and cast a coldness over the shepherds, and passed on, wolf-eyed.

The tavern door was shut and barred.

The shepherds beat their blue fists on the door. 'Open up, Fara!' they shouted. 'We're thirsty.' An English trooper went by and eyed them with contempt, and spat and passed on.

There was a notice on the door about enforced closure for the Twelve Days of Christmas; but the three shepherds couldn't read.

A small boy came out of the shadows and plucked old
Simon's sleeve.

'Follow me,' whispered the boy. He took the shepherds by
a garden path to a wicker gate they knew nothing about, and
down steps to another, hidden door.

The cellar was full of tobacco smoke and tallow reek from a
dozen candles stuck in empty flagons.

It took the Wideford shepherds a while to accustom their
eyes and recognise the fishermen and joiners and masons and
tinkers and labourers and layabouts inside.

A fiddle was playing softly.

A girl began to sing among the lasses preparing bread and
cheese and fish on a huge platter:

> Good be to this sturdy bigging!
> *We're a' St Mary's men*
> Fae the steethe stane to the rigging
> *Before Our Lady*.

The songs and the dancing went on till the candles were
burned out, and when the cellar doors were opened at last, the
late dawn light was coming in.

The three Wideford shepherds had not enjoyed such a night
since they were young men, thirty years before.

That they were celebrating in secret put an edge of danger
and delight on the ceremony.

They were not too clear as to how they got home, those old
Wideford shepherds, but they woke up in their bothy the next
morning, on the cold hill side.

★   ★   ★

On what would have been till lately 'the seventh day of Christmas,' two ships came sailing into the bay and dropped anchor.

A hundred English soldiers were ferried to the small piers from the first ship. They landed at the slipways and were marched in order to the courtyard of the provost's fine house, now the military barracks.

The colonel told those troopers that they would be going to billets in other islands and parishes, lest there be any royalists in such places capable of disturbing the new Cromwellian peace. They would be billeted in good farms, in Westray, Sanday, Rinansay, Stronsay, Rousay. Five-and-twenty soldiers would proceed immediately to Hamnavoe, a village in the west, where ships of every nation often sheltered from Atlantic storms; and so the sea folk of Hamnavoe were subject to all kinds of dangerous subversive rumours, such as that Charles Stuart, the Babylonish King of Great Britain, had not been judicially executed by the legally constituted parliament at all, but would wield great power, either him or his upstart son that had fled into France and had gotten sanctuary there. 'But,' cried the chaplain in the black coat, in his loud Levellers' voice, 'those Babylonish kings have been put down for ever – and their bishops and bells and golden candlesticks too …'

The skipper of the troop-ship Faith went to John Fara's tavern, and found it bolted and sign-posted. But presently the small boy plucked him by the sleeve.

*　*　*

In the early afternoon the second ship Hope began to discharge her cargo on to barges drawn up alongside out in the bay: a dozen heavy cannon, a forest of pikes, big fierce-looking clusters of musketry and (last) twenty terrified horses

168

that rolled their eyes like meteors and all but sunk the barges, stampending this way and that, till they were brought to land. The smell of grass and fresh water on the wind pacified them.

Soon the horses were led along the cobbles of the street to their stables in what had until lately been St Magnus Cathedral.

The skipper of the munitions ship read the notice prohibiting Christmas on Fara's door, and he shouted some fierce Norse words that the chaplain in the black coat would not have approved of.

But there he was at the angry skipper's shoulder, the boy, laughing, and he tugged at his sleeve and whispered a few Norn words into the skipper's ear.

★   ★   ★

Every waterfront, when large vessels anchor in the bay, is lined with idle curious people, until the cargoes are put ashore and crews follow with silver in their pockets, and their eyes throwing sealight and longing at the local lasses.

The two ships put ashore their munitions and reinforcements all that day, and it took till the midwinter sunset before the holds were empty.

'Oh yes indeed,' said the skippers of Faith and Hope to the colonel at the barracks gate, 'there is a third ship, Charity, but we lost her in that storm off Buchan Ness. She ran for shelter most like, in some harbour, Cromarty or Wick. She'll be here, for certain, tomorrow or the day after.'

'You should control your crews,' said Cromwell's chaplain severely. 'They are beginning to get out of hand.'

It turned out to be a very violent lawless day in Kirkwall.

The sailors were angry that the tavern was shut. They were tired and thirsty after a fortnight on the salt wastes of the German Ocean.

There has always been antipathy between sailors and soldiers. The trouble began when the sergeant on duty forbade the crews to share the meagre barrack refreshments. 'Soldiers only,' be said, 'soldiers who know how to drink soberly and solemnly. No drunken ships' rabble in Cromwell's barracks. Besides, the beer is thin and strictly rationed.'

That started it. Fists flew, stones were flung, eyes were blued and blacked, noses were ruined red taps, windows were smashed, panels splintered, there had never been such coarse language (and in all the tongues of Europe) on the quiet streets of Kirkwall.

Even the voice of Cromwell's chaplain counselling peace, was drowned in those surging seas of wrath and blood.

Some say it was the fiercest battle in Orkney since Summerdale a century before.

Others say, that street fight was the origin of the famous Ba' game that is still played in the streets of Kirkwall; but the game is much much older, and had its origin perhaps in the struggle of the elemental giants, Ice and Fire, for possession of the life-kindling sun, at midwinter.

At last, somehow, the knot of soldiers and sailors was disentangled with the pikes and pistols of the garrison.

A few soldiers and seamen were put in the rough infirmary, and bandaged; a few were put in the lock-up of the barracks, and buckets of icy water were thrown over them.

* * *

And still, all that tenth day, there was no sign of the third ship in the convoy, Charity.

The black-coat chaplain uttered grim prognostications.

The Kirkwall townsfolk, most of them, went home in twos and threes, sated with excitement and terror. This was not the kind of Yule Ba' game they were accustomed to!

170

A few townsfolk went in secret to the side-door of St Magnus, to celebrate in silence and candle-light the seventh day of Yule, when the three magi brought gifts of gold and frankincense and myrrh to the infant King of the universe.

And a few went to the secret cellar door of Fara's hostelry. The linker girl was singing in her sweet pure voice, the townsmen and the two skippers gave back the surging chorus:

> This night is good New Year's night
> *Were a' St Mary's men*
> And we've come here to crave our right
> *Before our Lady.*
>
> We'll tell you how our queen is drest
> *We're a' St Mary's men*
> If you will gi'e us o' your best
> *Before Our Lady ...*

* * *

A small company of troopers, under a corporal, had been billeted in the sea village of Hamnavoe on the west side of the island, fifteen miles away.

The next morning this corporal rode into the barracks from Hamnavoe.

The corporal reported that a ship had anchored in the roadstead the evening before. Her sails were torn, a few spars broken. She had come through a bad storm, obviously.

The skipper had made no attempt to communicate with the laird or with the small garrison.

Nothing at all seemed to be happening on this strange ship.

About midnight a lantern was observed on the ship's side. Two shadowy people – one a woman carrying a child – were handed down into a small ship's boat, and rowed ashore by a sailor, a black man.

The passengers were put ashore at a small stone jetty. They had little in the way of luggage.

The man has asked the way to the inn, but the fishermen told them the inn was closed till the Twelve Days of Christmas were over. Today was Twelfth Night.

The inn would be open again for guests at midnight, maybe: for, said the fishermen, 'it's hard cruel hungry times in the world now, and the soldiers are like Pharaoh's locusts, eating and drinking everything ...'

The negro chanted in a dark rich voice from the slipway where he was holding the rope, *Behold your King cometh*.

It was beautiful, that voice, in the star-crowned night.

The corporal told the colonel, 'Sir, perhaps I ought to have interrogated these people, and the negro too, with his talk or a King returning. But, that quiet night of stars and silver snowfall, they looked to be peaceable folk. So I let them walk away out of the village into the night. There is a shebeen here and there in the countryside where they might get shelter ... Only I thought it best to ride to Kirkwall with this strange news ... The name of the ship in Hamnavoe harbour? Sir, she's called Charity.'

The Sons of Upland Farm

A farmer on the island of Hoy had three sons.

His wife died in middle age. But Adam the farmer said, 'This farm has been in our family for six generations. I have seen it grow from a poor hill croft in my grandfather's time to the most fertile farm in the parish. Now it doesn't matter how soon I follow my wife into the kirkyard. There are three sons. The inheritance is secure.'

The farmer had a share in a ship that traded out of Hamnavoe in Orkney to the Baltic.

He said one day to William, the eldest son, 'I think you should sail in our ship *Heatherbell* on her next voyage. I don't altogether trust the skipper. The profits have been down for three voyages past. Keep an eye on the bills of lading and the waterfront exchanges. Then be back in time for harvest.'

His son William joined the ship at Hamnavoe at midsummer. He got on well with the skipper and the crew. Once the cargo of salted herring – two hundred barrels – was under hatches, the ship sailed with a fair wind and tide through Scapa Flow.

Neither ship nor crew was ever seen again.

It was known there had been an easterly storm in the North Sea, that had damaged many ships.

The *Heatherbell,* it seemed, had been lost with all hands

II

The second son was called Jamie.

He was a hard-working young man and when he was still a boy he knew most things about work on a big farm. It was said he knew the 'horseman's word,' that could make the most intractable horse gentle and biddable.

The farmer employed several farm servants, men and girls. He drove them hard – he sometimes struck one or other if they did something stupid or perverse – but he paid them a higher fee than the other farmers, and he saw to it that they were well fed and housed.

His sons he treated more roughly than the servants.

He said one day to Jamie, 'I've bought a horse from a farm in Aberdeenshire. You're to go tomorrow to fetch the horse here. Don't delay by as much as one night. Here's your fare. They'll feed you at the farm in Aberdeenshire.'

The second son said there was to be a meeting of the island Horsemen's Society, and they were expecting him to help with initiations in the great Bu barn, the next night.

'You'll take the ferry south to Scotland,' said the farmer, 'in the morning.'

So Jamie set out from Hamnavoe.

The farmer expected son and horse back within the week. When a fortnight had come and gone, he began to be worried.

He wrote a letter to the horse-dealer, asking if his son Jamie had taken the horse, according to the bargain.

The horse-dealer sent no answer. (Horse-dealers in those days rarely put pen to paper. The spoken word, the struck hand,

174

drams taken, the exchange of a few sovereigns – that was the only kind of communication they understood.)

But half a year later the farmer did get a letter, from Jamie. 'Dear Father, It might as the Good Book says be a good thing for the eyes to behold the sun, and young men are bidden to rejoice in their youth, but there has been little joy in your farm since our mother died, and the sun does not shine on your fields and labourers as it does on the oat-fields of other farmers. I write to say that I will not return to Hoy. The horse you bought is still with the dealer. I met in the Mearns a bonny kind lass, a tattie-picker from Ireland, and I have settled there with her and we are married and I am farm manager to a rich landlord who lives in London and attends the Parliament there.'

III

The farmer lit his pipe with this letter and said, 'Life gets more interesting the older you get. But you have to harden your heart like a stone. Tom, you'll have to sharpen *your* ideas, my lad. I'm gray and bent. There's the heavy burden of this farm on you in the years to come, and you with the wits of a scarecrow.'

Tom was the third son.

He was the strangest boy the island had known for a long time.

It was not that Tom was work-shy. He could do whatever he was told, such as dig peats or stumble after an ox at ploughtime, or sink creels for lobsters. But he could do nothing by himself. He had to be shown what to do, and then he did the work, not well, but passably. The prospect of him operating this big farm after his father was dust was unthinkable. It was very hurtful to the old man.

Tom was very good at imitating the songs of birds and all animal sounds. Half-way down a furrow, he would stop and speak awhile to the ox, like two friends conversing. But he was best of all at imitating the speech of the island folk, for everyone had a different way of speaking, and Tom had the tune and the rhythm of their talk to perfection. Everyone laughed except the person being imitated, who would generally be glum for a whole day after. (But this person had, always, done something to disrupt the harmony of the parish.)

But what good are bird calls and satire on a farm, especially a rich important farm like Upland?

The old farmer looked at his son and shook his head.

Next Lammas fair at Hamnavoe, all the farm workers in Hoy had the day off, as every year. They went in half a dozen skiffs to Hamnavoe, and Tom sailed with them. 'Keep an eye on the creature!' said the farmer. 'It wouldn't make that much difference if he disappeared, like his brothers. But still, a father needs some kin to close his eyes. I hope Tom finds some good hard-working country lass at the fair.'

When the six skiffs sailed back to Hoy in late evening, Tom wasn't there.

'There was a troupe of play-actors in Hamnavoe,' said the Hoy shepherd to the farmer. 'There was a hurdy-gurdy man and a man who threw burning knives all round a lass, and a monkey in a cage. They sang the latest London songs. It cost sixpence to get in. I didn't go. But I saw Tom going in. Tom wasn't at the pier when we foregathered at sundown to sail home. Maybe he fell asleep in the pub. He'll be home in the morning with a sore head.'

'I expect the play-actors have taken him for a side-show,' said the old farmer.

IV

The next winter the farmer died.

Then slowly the farm went to pieces.

The farm servants feed themselves to other farms. A fourth cousin of the farmer, a Kirkwall solicitor the farmer had never once spoken to, claimed to inherit the land and stock and dwellings. At once he put them on the market.

But the islanders were chary of purchasing, for the lost sons might turn up some day, and demand their inheritance.

The farm remained unsold. Doors and shutters warped. The roofs began to fall in. The meadowland was full of rushes. Bad boys out for a lark on Hallowe'en night sent stones splintering through the windows, leaving black stars.

The rabbits made burrows under the ploughland.

The plough at the barn wall was flaky with rust, then that powerful share was completely eaten with the slow red fire.

V

The little hotel in the village twelve miles away closed its guest rooms in winter, once the English grouse-shooters and trout-fishers went home. Only the bar room stayed open for the convenience of the islanders.

A half-dozen men were drinking at the fire one bitter cold winter night.

Suddenly the door opened and three strangers came in, shaking snow from their capes. They set down their boxes and trunks.

The landlord was about to say his house was closed for the winter, when the huge foreign-looking man with the red beard and the ring in his ear rang three gold sovereigns on the counter and requested three rooms for the night.

A sovereign in those days was a large fee.

The landlord put the coins in his till and listened to the rich music it made among the pennies and farthings.

Then the landlord opened his register and the three guests signed, one after another.

'Now, gentlemen,' said the landlord, 'what can I get you this cold night?'

The gruff red-beard who had signed himself as 'Merchant and Shipowner' said, 'I hear they make good whisky among the hills here. Bring three glasses of Hoy malt.'

The strangers went over and sat by themselves at the window seat. The window was crammed with stars, until the next snow shower blotted them out, and after that the stars were out again, a winter swarm in the deep purple.

The island men, after a silence, began to discuss the island news, such as it was.

One said there had still been no legal settlement about Upland Farm. It was a sorrowful thing, to see a prosperous farm in ruins.

A girl at the other end of the island — it seemed — had been put out of the farm she worked in, on account of 'her condition.' The farmer had told her to go to the Inspector of Poor in the village. He might be able to give her a shilling or two to get by on, or direct her to the poorhouse in Kirkwall. To stay on as butter-and-cheese lass at his farm, he declared, was impossible.

The girl had knocked at this door and that, and been given a cup of milk or a scone, but no one had offered to take her in.

'Now,' said the landlord, 'I was having my afternoon snooze in the rocking-chair, when I thought I heard a knock at the door. But it must have been a snowfall from the roof, or the fire sinking.'

'Well,' said the shepherd, 'I saw that lass wandering across the hill after sunset. I called after her, she was welcome to bide at our fire. But a blizzard muffled my shout. When the blizzard passed, there was no one to be seen.'

'God help anybody out on a night like this,' said the blacksmith.

'Well,' said the shopkeeper, 'but they bring it on themselves.'

'Now, gentlemen,' said the landlord to the rich guests, 'my wife has a pot of good Scotch broth on the fire, and there's steak and clapshot, whenever you're ready.'

The black-bearded guest who had signed himself in as 'Landowner' – and a prosperous keeper of flocks and herds he seemed – said they had an errand to do first, then they would return for their supper, maybe after midnight.

'The roads are drifted under. Will I send the boy to go before you with a lantern?' said the landlord.

The youngest of the strangers, who had signed in as 'Poet,' said they would find their way by the stars. 'When a child is born,' he said, 'there is one star kindled to light the soul on its journey . . .' The poet, unlike his two companions, was rather poorly clad for winter, in an old patched coat and moleskin trousers. Out of his pocket stuck a penny whistle. He was much the merriest of the three. But often he paused upon a thought, and then his gravity seemed to be a deeper pool than the austere looks of his companions.

They got to their feet, all three, at the same time.

'Might I ask, where exactly are the gentlemen bound for?' asked the landlord.

They said nothing. They shouldered their boxes. They walked out into a new flurry of snow.

'I think they're government men,' said the gravedigger. 'From the excise. You should never have sold them that home-made whisky.'

The landlord said he wasn't afraid of that.

They heard, between two surges of snow, a scatter of notes from the road-end. The third stranger, the poet, the patched one, was playing on his tin whistle.

'Look in the register,' said the shepherd. 'See what their names are.'

The names were William Adamson, James Adamson and Thomas Adamson, of Upland Farm in Hoy, Orkney.

★　★　★

It was near midnight when the heirs of Upland arrived at the ruined farm.

All was silence, darkness, desolation.

But in the byre where the cattle had wintered long ago, they saw a feeble light.

Someone had stuck a candle in an empty bottle.

It seemed to be earth's tremulous answer to the star of the Nativity.

One by one the travellers walked towards the glimmering cowshed.

Dialogue at the Year's End

'I've been out all this short day,' said the old cripple woman in the straw chair by the fire. 'I was keeping the ways clear between the house and the barn and the byre and the stable. I shovelled and shovelled till the snow stood higher than myself. Sometimes I was half blinded with the brightness.'

'If you aren't a wonder,' said the apple-faced child in the door.

'What can anybody do in February?' said the old done woman with the grey shawl muffling her mouth. 'Oh but my needles went clickety-clack, clickety-clack, and a jumper with bonny patterns brown and white fell from the knitting needles. I'll be the bonniest lass at the barn dance at the Bu come the weekend. I will.'

'No gull was ever so busy,' said the flame-bright boy, and put another peat on the fire.

'Oh,' said the old wife on two sticks, 'they're the lazy ones, men. A bit of a blow from the west, a wave or two clashing on the shore, and it's too stormy for the sea. *Up and off with you,* I cried this morning, *there's a thousand cod off Yesnaby* . . . The one that's to be my man come harvest, he was the first to push out. The *Gannet,* that's the name of his boat. They followed, one after another. By sunset today I was gutting a hundred fish.'

'This place would starve without you,' said the grass-green boy.

'I'm always one to keep a bonny house,' said the old grannie in a voice like withered grass. 'So after porridge time, I found seven stone jars in the cupboard. Ah, it was bonny today on the hill. I came home with my apron brimming with buttercups and daisies and long sweet grasses. I filled the jars and I set them here and there about the house. I took the loan of daffodils from the grieve's garden. The daffodils I put in water in a jar in the window.'

'You make everything bright that you touch,' said the child with flower-sweet skin.

'I forget what I did today,' said the old dame with chin whiskers. 'I'm beginning to forget things. Oh now I know – I made ale. I steeped a hundredweight of malt and a I threw in brown sugar, handful on handful, and I added the barm. And oh! I nearly forgot – I poured in a jar of honey. There will never be a more noble head of froth in this island, never, nowhere. There's a hundred reels and dances in that ale. It will drive the fiddlers mad. Men will tell stories about this brew of mine. It's to be for a certain wedding.'

'This island is happy for you alone,' said the boy with loch-blue eyes.

'Well, what a day this has been!' said she of the toothless mouth. 'We gathered the kindling all week. We went in one long line, with loaded shoulders up the hill. We poured in fat and fish oil.

At midnight the laird lit the fire – his face was red with port wine and flames. Fifty young shadows sang and danced through the flames. At sunrise, even the jealous ones agreed, I and a certain boy were the best pair of dancers round the midsummer fire.'

'I hope he kissed you,' said the child with a white butterfly in his fingers.

'A day is so short,' said the old wife with cindery breath. 'I think I waited at some grand table today, candles and bottles of wine and a silver plate with salmon and a silver plate with grouse. But was it the Manse or the Hall or the Hamnavoe provost's house? Wherever it was, a fine man said across his wineglass, *Everything tastes sweeter because of the waitress.* Hanks of cigar-smoke hung over the table. I wouldn't change my fisherman for him, gold watch-chain and cigar and fine high chant.'

'You're better than any lady in London,' said the boy with honey strands between his fingers.

'I can't talk of tiredness,' said the rattle of bone-and-stick from the rocking-chair. 'I think I was never so tired. My body is veined with the heavy gold of harvest. From rise of sun to rose of sunset we laboured. I followed the flame and flash of a certain scythe, I bent and I bound the scatterings of gold like Ruth. The corncrakes creaked. The bees trudged home with their own pure gold. At noon the women poured bottles of ale in a jug, and they spread bannocks with golden butter. One young harvester snored against a stook, his head humming like a hive. I shook him awake, but gently.'

'You're the golden girl,' said the child with the ear of corn twined in his hair.

'Oh this, this,' said the old dreamer, her face laved in flame-shadows, 'this was the very happiest day of my life. First thing,

I washed in sweet cold water. Then the girls swathed me about in a heavy whiteness. Then we followed the fiddler, a long long column, from my father's croft to the kirk. The minister came with his book and we stood before him, the man and me, and he put the gold ring on my shivering finger – look. Then we followed the fiddle home. The man threw pennies to the parish boys. The world came to the wedding – the cows and the horses, the grass and the clouds and the waves, the sun followed us in through the door, and when I looked through the skylight, the stars had come to the wedding, and the moon put silver coins on the loch for the wedding. Where are you now? Why don't you speak to me, man?'

'A stone is generally silent,' said the boy with the blackbird breath.

'The silence was hardest of all to bear,' sighed the old woman with webs at her mouth. 'Today the silence crushed me like quernstones. That silence box-long on the trestles. Then the figures in black one by one coming to my chair, and pausing, and going on out. The silence borne away by eight black silences. Then the black silent shawls of the neighbours about me, in a slow dark silent dance, all day. The last one lit the lamp and left. Silent they drifted across the pane, first snowflakes. I woke in this chair by the dead fire. The room was bright with snow and dawn.'

'The swan's silent too,' cried the silver voice of the child beside the snowman.

'I was never so happy and never so tired,' cried the swan princess, flying between the hill and the loch with a sun-cake in its beak. 'Where must I fly with this sun-cake? I took it from the hand of a boy who stood in a poor croft door, it was yellow with barley and honey, it was warm from peatsmoke and flame.

184

Where should I take the sun-cake that is baked on the hearth in the depths of winter, when the wick of the sun burns low and cold in the south? My wings are heavy, the loch is frozen over.'

'To the poorest house in the world,' chimed the crystal in the throat of the child. 'Go out, old grandmother now through the snow, with the suncakes in your basket.'

Sources

Books by GMB: [*AOS*] *Andrina and Other Stories* (London: Chatto and Windus/Hogarth Press, 1983). — [*CS*] *Christmas Stories* (Oxford: Perpetua Press, 1985). — [*CT*] *Christmas Tales* (Lastingham: Celtic Cross Press, 2010). — [*MF*] *The Masked Fisherman and Other Stories* (London: John Murray, 1989). — [*PM*] *The Poor Man in His Castle* (Lastingham: Celtic Cross Press, 2004. — [*WE*] *Weihnachtsgäste: Erzählungen*, trans. Esther Garke (Frauenfeld, Switzerland: Verlag Im Waldgut, 1990). — [*WT*] *Winter Tales* (London: John Murray, 1995).

'Anna's Boy': *Tablet* (24/31 December 1988), *MF*, *WE*.

'The Box of Fish': *Scotsman*, *AOS*, *WE*.

'A Candle for Milk and Grass': *Glasgow Herald* (December 1976), *AOS*, *WE*.

'The Children's Feast': *Tablet* (23/30 December 1989); *CS*, *WE*, *WT*.

'A Child's Christmas': *Tablet* (19/26 December 1987).

'The Christmas Dove': *Tablet* (19/26 December 1981), *CS*, *MF*, *WE*.

'The Christmas Exile': *Edinburgh Evening News* (28 December 1983).

'The Christmas Horse': *Glasgow Herald*, (24 December 1988); *CT*.

'A Christmas Story': *Orcadian* (25 December 1950), *RD*. 'Christmas Visitors': *CS*, *MF*, *WE*.

'Croft in January': *MF*, *WE*.

'Darkness and Light': *Scotsman* (December 1976), *AOS*, *MF*, *WE*.

'Dialogue at the Year's End': *Scotsman* (31 December 1968), *MF*.

'An Epiphany Tale': *Scottish Field*, AOS, *WE*. 'The Feast of the Strangers: An Orkney Fable': *Scotsman* (21 December 1974).

'A Haul of Winter Fish': *Scotsman* (December 1983), *MF*, *CS*, *WE*.

'Herman: A Christmas Story': *Glasgow Herald* (23 December 1989).

'I Saw Three Ships': *Scotsman on Sunday* [*Spectrum* magazine] (22 December 1996).

'The Last Island Boy: A Story for Christmas': *Scotsman* (24 December 1985), *WE*.

'The Lost Boy': *Scotsman* (December 1981), *AOS*, *WE*.

'The Lost Sheep': *Tablet* (22/29 December 1990), *WT*.

'The Lost Traveller': *Tablet* (24/31 December 1994).

'Miss Tait and Tommy and the Carol Singers': *CS*, *MF*, *WE*.

'The Nativity: A Story for Yule': *New Shetlander* (December 1948).

'The Old Man in the Snow': *Scotsman* (December 1984), *CT*.

'One Christmas in Birsay': typescript dated 16–17 November 1987 (Orkney Library D124/175/5).

'The Poor Man in His Castle': *PM*. 'The Sons of Upland Farm': *Daily Telegraph* (December 1994), *WT*.

'Stars': *Tablet* (23/30 December 1995), *CT*.

'The Three Old Men': *Tablet* (21/28 December 1991), *WT*.

'The Winter Song': *Scotsman* (27 December 1980), *MF*.

We are grateful to David Mackey, Senior Archivist at the Orkney Library and Archive, for supplying copies of several of the stories.